I0417866

In the Valley of Lily

Katja Doremus

Copyright © 2015 Katja Doremus
All rights reserved.
ISBN: 0990959511
ISBN-13: 978-0990959519
Cover Image : marinomarini/shutterstock

DEDICATION

for S.B.

CONTENTS

ACKNOWLEDGMENTS

There are so many people who have helped me along the way. My amazing editors, Bethany Stone and Danielle van B, for your kind words of encouragement every time I start to panic and threaten to toss it all. Wendy and Claire from Bare Naked Words, for all the hard work they did in helping get this weird little book out there. My gorgeous roommate, who has put up with dirty teacups scattered around the house for months – I promise I'll try to be better! My family, for always supporting me, even when I'm doing something completely insane, like writing erotica. And my friends. I love you all so very much and I never could have done this without you.

PART ONE

1

Lily arrived by train with only a small rolling suitcase. As promised, a car waited to take her to Chateau Oriol, where she would be working for the summer.

The driver leaned against the car, smoking a cigarette, and watched as she made her way across the deserted parking lot, dragging her bag behind her. When she approached, he dropped the cigarette, crushing it beneath his shoe, and wordlessly took Lily's suitcase. He then opened the back door, and Lily slid inside.

She stared out the window as he navigated the twisting roads leading from the village nestled in the Pyrenees. This was her first time abroad and she promised herself that she would remember every detail. As the car picked up speed, leaving the village behind, Lily caught sight of a stream in the valley below, the water shimmering like the belly of a fish.

They drove in silence. The driver kept his eyes on the road in front of him. The landscape here was wild and verdant. Dark pine forests covered the mountainsides.

Circling above one peak, a hawk spread its wings in search of prey.

Time stood still.

Only when the driver pulled in front of an ornate wrought-iron gate did Lily realize they had arrived. A tall stone wall surrounded the property, ancient and covered in a blanket of lichen and moss.

There, emblazoned on a bronze plaque tinged green with time, was the name. Chateau Oriol. Lily leaned forward as the driver rolled down the window and punched the keys on a discrete keypad. For a second, a hint of lavender caught in the breeze and then, just as quickly, the gate swung open and the driver rolled up his window.

The driveway curved around an open field, wild, untamed, and then, before them, rose the house. Chateau Oriol. Lily's lips parted in amazement.

The driver opened her door and then he took her suitcase, depositing it on the gravel before returning to the car. He drove off without ever saying a word and Lily watched him speed around the bend and disappear from sight.

The sun beat down on her pale cheeks as she lifted her face to the sky and breathed in the fresh mountain air, inhaling the sweet perfume of lavender and the dry, brittle scent of pine.

She heard, in the distance, a dog barking.

Lily took her bag and went up the steps to the front door. When she'd seen the job posting, Maid needed for three months in Spanish summer villa, she'd hastily applied, hoping for an opportunity to leave her life behind and with it, everything she knew.

She'd imagined a beach town, terra cotta roofs and white washed stucco. She'd imagined olive groves and Spanish sunshine.

She had not envisioned these remote mountains near the French border or this house of grey stone, its fortress-like walls punctuated by large, shuttered windows, that towered over her.

Two weeks ago, a one-way ticket arrived by mail. She spent the last of her savings on five days in Madrid. There, she ate paella and visited the Prado and the Reina Sofía, feeling elegant and worldly as she admired *Guernica* and Goya's Black Paintings. Saturn, ripping the flesh from his son, had repulsed her just as it captivated her. She spent a long time standing there, torn between disgust and fascination.

Just the memory of those five days was enough for Lily to give up her summer to scrub floors.

After tucking her long blond hair behind her ears, she knocked on the massive front door, its dark wood scratched and scarred by time and age. Lily found herself running her fingertips over the grooves as if it were the battle-scarred skin of a loved one.

When no one answered, she searched for a doorbell but there was none. Just a heavy brass knocker, which she lifted and let fall with a hollow thud.

A sharp wind swept through the mountain pass, making Lily shiver. She glanced at her surroundings, the twisted pines in the distance, the lavender that seemed to cover everything, its olive-grey leaves and dusty purple blooms coloring the landscape. It was a rugged landscape, harsh and uninviting. And yet, here and there, if she looked closely, she noticed a brightly colored flower or the wings of a beautiful butterfly. As if such beauty could only survive in hiding.

She turned back to the door, worried there had been some misunderstanding. What if they weren't expecting her today? What if this was not the house? But that couldn't be. The driver had been waiting for her at the train station, just as they had promised.

Try as she might, she could not hear cars passing on the road just beyond the high wall. As though, upon entering the grounds, the world had ceased to be.

Just as panic gripped her, the door creaked open to reveal a trim man in his sixties. His thick white hair gave him a slightly patrician air that contrasted with his practical work clothes. He squinted at her, as if surprised to see her standing there at all.

"You're late," he said gruffly, holding the door open for Lily to enter.

Surprised he didn't offer to help with her bag, Lily gripped the handle, gritted her teeth, and stepped across the threshold.

Cool air that smelled faintly of stone and dust washed over her. When her eyes became accustomed to the shadowy light and she could make out her surroundings, her mouth fell open.

She stood at the threshold of a magnificent room, so grand it made her think of a cathedral. The floors were covered in elaborately patterned tiles, faded with time and the passing of generations of feet, but no less beautiful for it.

If anything, age added to their splendor.

The man did not inquire about her trip. Instead, he started in without preamble.

"Tardiness will not be tolerated. Mr. Darby is very particular in that regard. First, I will show you the house. You are expected to keep it in perfect order. Usually, it will just be the three of us here, plus the cook during the day. However, Mr. Darby holds a number of parties over the summer and you are to care for each of his guests as if they were the master of the house. Understood?"

Lily nodded, too awed to listen carefully to his words. For if she had been listening more closely, she might have noticed his peculiar tone. But the chateau was truly breathtaking and Lily could not focus her attention both on the house and on the man before her.

Sconces mounted high on the walls cast an eerie light over everything. Still, even in shadows, the house was enchanting.

An enormous staircase stood before her, the mahogany banisters polished and gleaming. And to her right, a grand fireplace, so tall she could easily have stood in it without stooping. There, above the fireplace, hung a portrait of a beautiful, dark haired woman reclining on a gold settee. Her lips wore a peculiar smile that made Lily blush, as if she were privy to something much more personal and private than the portrait actually depicted.

Hypnotized by the painting, Lily did not notice the man abruptly stop. She collided with him, causing him to curse in anger.

"I'm sorry," she apologized, her voice swallowed up by the cavernous room.

He gave her a dark look before glancing quickly at the painting. "He will call you girl if he needs to call you anything at all. Do not bother him with personal information. He is uninterested." He paused for a moment before adding, almost under his breath, "Mr. Darby is famous for his temper."

Looking around, Lily wondered, not for the last time, if she had made a terrible mistake in coming here. No one knew where she was. She had no one to tell. Only her mother, who was happy to finally be rid of her.

"Your day begins at six and ends whenever Mr. Darby is finished with you. Most evenings, you will be free to return to your room after dinner has been cleared. However, if he has guests, you will be expected to be available until they retire. Sundays you are free to do as you please. If you would like to go into the village, it can likely be arranged."

They passed through the large entry hall and continued down a narrow corridor. He pointed out the rooms on each side, powder room, library, office, but did not stop. And then he threw open a door to reveal a grand sitting room, decorated in cream linen and gold. Light spilled through the muslin curtains, illuminating dust motes in the air, and making Lily wonder if this room, for all its beauty, was ever used.

Pointing to the French doors lining one wall, he said, "The south terrace. Mr. Darby occasionally takes his coffee there." With that, they returned to the corridor. "Your room is on the third floor, in the servants quarters. After you put down your things, I will introduce you to Mr. Darby. Always address him as sir."

"Of course." Lily could hardly wait to meet the man who owned such a spectacular home.

"The kitchen is through there. This is the servants' stairway. You are not to use the main staircase unless directed."

The chateau, and all its rules, felt so foreign, so ancient to Lily. And she wondered if this was how things were done here. The formal use of sir. The servants.

Unaccustomed to such formalities, Lily asked the man his name.

He paused, one foot on the step to the narrow staircase, and turned to look at her. He held her gaze longer than necessary and Lily felt the judgment in his dark eyes.

"Tomas," he said finally.

He did not offer her his hand nor did he ask for her name in return. She nodded and then struggled with her bag up the cramped staircase. Dim light bulbs cast an eerie glow over the wallpapered walls. She could make out tiny flowers, faded by age and time.

By the time they reached the third floor, Lily was panting. Tomas did not wait for her to catch her breath. He hurried down the corridor, forcing Lily to trudge behind him.

He stopped abruptly and removed a heavy set of keys from his pocket and unlocked a plain, unmarked door.

Peering over his shoulder, Lily saw the single wrought-iron bed with one blanket tossed over it. A plain pine wardrobe. And a small window high on the wall. That was all. The utilitarian room, without a touch of warmth, reminded Lily of a monastery.

Still, though small, it was larger than her room back home.

"Do you live here?" Lily asked, glancing at the doors lining both sides of the narrow corridor.

Tomas peered down his nose at her. "I live in the carriage house."

"Oh." The thought that she was all alone here scared Lily slightly, though she would never have admitted it. But the truth was, at eighteen, she was still frightened of the dark.

Lily knew it was childish, but she could not shake the feeling that the house was haunted. So many empty rooms and dark corners.

She shivered.

Tomas turned towards her, looking her up and down and Lily shrank back, instantly disliking the way his humorless eyes felt on her skin.

"Do you have a dress?" he asked, clearly displeased with what he was seeing.

She nodded. She'd packed several summer dresses, expecting a villa in the sun. Not a mansion surrounded by dark forests and mountains.

"Good. Change. I will wait here."

With that, he stepped outside, yanking the door shut behind him, causing it to rattle on its frame.

She looked around at the poor furnishings, noting the familiar scent of mothballs that reminded her of her grandmother, a stern woman who had died not long before.

Unzipping her suitcase, Lily wondered what kind of man would live alone in such a large and uninviting house, with only a maid and a manservant for company.

She'd find out soon enough.

2

"Address him as sir," Tomas repeated as they traversed another long corridor. Carpets muffled their footfalls. And then he stopped, knocking twice on a heavy mahogany door. He stepped aside, forcing Lily to inch past him.

The door closed behind her with an ominous click.

"For the love of god, girl, come closer. I can't see you when you're skulking in the shadows," a stern voice barked out, making Lily jump.

Enormous windows flooded the room with light. Worn Persian carpets in elegant red and blue patterns covered most of the hardwood floor and the walls were lined with leather bound books.

Behind a large desk sat a man watching her with hawk-like eyes. He wore a pale blue oxford, the top buttons undone, the sleeves pushed up, giving Lily the impression that he had been hard at work until she'd interrupted. His brown hair was brushed back from his handsome face.

To Lily, it was the face of a man who belonged in a house such as this. Regal. Stern.

She guessed him to be in his early forties.

He tapped his fingers on the desk. "You must be the American," he said at last, leaning forward. He frowned then added, "Do you always stand like that?"

"What?"

"Am I not speaking clearly enough?" he enunciated each word as if he thought she was deaf or dumb while she just stared at him, too shocked to respond. "Do. You. Always. Stand. Like. That?"

"I guess?" She straightened up, suddenly worried that she had travelled all this way only to be shown the door.

He picked up the phone and barked out an order in Spanish before slamming it down in its cradle and glaring at Lily. "Your posture is appalling. You look like a scared little puppy afraid you'll get another kick in the stomach. For the love of god, stand up straight!"

Lily pushed her shoulders back and lifted her chin.

"Better. Your appearance reflects on this house and I will not tolerate you looking ghastly. Is that clear?"

"Yes, sir," she said meekly. It felt strange, addressing him as sir, but she did it anyway, hoping to appease him. She caught the hint of a smile, gone so quickly she thought moments later that maybe she'd imagined it.

"Your passport." He held out his hand.

"It's upstairs," she stammered. "I can go get it."

"Don't be stupid. TOMAS!"

The door opened and Lily turned to see Tomas standing there, wearing a sardonic expression.

"Her passport."

"Of course, sir." Tomas departed, pulling the door shut once more.

"Before you begin, there are several documents you

will need to sign. Sit if you'd like."

He waved dismissively at the straight-backed chair in front of the desk, like he couldn't care less if she sat or stood for the remainder of the day.

She sat, clasping her hands on her lap to keep from trembling. Had she really been so naïve as to expect a kindly reception?

He studied her in silence, the pinched look on his face giving the impression that he had just caught a whiff of something putrid.

Finally, nodding to himself, he pushed a stack of papers across the desk.

"I won't have my privacy compromised because some foolish girl decides to have a few pints. If you are unwilling to sign a confidentiality agreement, Tomas will take you back to the train station immediately."

Lily shook her head, causing her hair to fall loosely around her face. "That's not a problem."

She didn't want him to know how desperately she needed this job, but the truth was, without it, she'd be lost. He'd paid only for the ticket to Spain and she didn't have the money to buy a ticket home.

Not that she wanted to go home. There was nothing waiting for her there.

"Very well. The next document details the terms of your employment. Read them both and sign them."

A knock on the door interrupted them and then Tomas appeared silently, placing her passport on the desk in front of Mr. Darby. Lily blushed, imagining him riffling through her suitcase, seeing all her carefully folded underwear. Mr. Darby glanced quickly at her passport before standing. He opened a safe in the wall and, glancing over his shoulder, said simply, "It will be safer here than in your room."

Mr. Darby sat back and continued to stare openly at her. Even as she scanned the confidentiality agreement, Lily felt his eyes on her, assessing her, judging her.

Knowing that keeping his secrets would not be an issue, Lily read quickly, comprehending only a fraction of detailed legal document in front of her.

"Do you have a pen?"

Without a word, he produced a beautiful ballpoint pen and for a moment, Lily stared at the majestic writing implement, knowing it likely cost more than everything she owned combined.

Smooth ink sailed across the page as she signed her name and dated it.

"Terms of your employment," Mr. Darby said gruffly, pushing another stack of papers towards her.

She read quickly, feeling a prick of worry when she realized that payment would only be made upon the completion of her time at the chateau. Still, she knew she could not object, so when she reached the final page, finding nothing too troublesome, she signed her name once more.

Mr. Darby glanced impatiently at his wrist. "We'll see how long you last. The girl before you left after a week." He nodded once more to himself. "The doctor is waiting. You may go."

There had been no mention of a doctor exam, either before her arrival, or in the paperwork she'd read, but Lily did not have the courage to argue. It surprised her even more to see that the chateau had a medical suite on the first floor. A bright room with stark white walls and an exam table. The doctor introduced himself as Charles Dalton and smiled at her. She hated doctors, and while she didn't understand the necessity of a physical, she knew instinctively she had no place to object. Not when Mr. Darby had her passport in his safe and so clearly thought she would fail before the week was out.

She refused to give him the satisfaction of being right.

"This won't take long," the doctor was saying, smiling down at Lily while she sat at the end of the exam table. The paper made a dry crackling sound every time she moved so she tried to stay as still as possible.

He'd already taken her weight and height, her blood pressure and all the rest. Noting in her file that she would be starting school in the fall, he'd also assured her that he would get her up to date with her vaccinations. "No reason you should have to go through this ordeal again in a couple of months," he'd said patting her knee.

She'd taken to him immediately. The doctor appeared to be roughly the age of Mr. Darby, but whereas Mr. Darby was stern, the doctor was always smiling, which put Lily quickly at ease.

She felt safe in this brightly lit room with the doctor.

So when he told her that he would need to do a complete exam, she did not protest. She did, however, inform him, blushing slightly and stammering, that she was a virgin and had never before had an exam of this nature.

For a moment, the doctor paused, a crease forming between his eyebrows, causing Lily to wonder if she'd made a mistake in telling him. She chided herself for being silly. After all, he would certainly realize she was a virgin once he'd examined her.

Finally, he gave her a radiant smile. "I promise to be as

gentle as possible."

For some reason, Lily believed him, and so, while the doctor waited in the hall, she changed into a cloth gown, and then, leaned back on the table and squeezed her eyes closed, willing her heart to stop racing.

After the exam, the doctor produced a tight fitting brace to help improve Lily's posture. It looked to Lily like a corset, with eyelets in the front and laces in the back. It fit around her torso, covering her small breasts, and cinching her waist.

The doctor stood behind her and instructed her to grip the exam table for support. Lily grunted when he yanked the strings tight, forcing the air from her lungs.

Once he was satisfied that it was tied as tight as needed, the doctor told Lily she could stand up and turn around. She did, blushing, feeling ridiculous trussed as she was.

"You may find it necessary to breathe out of your nose instead of your mouth." He jotted something down in her file before looking up at her again. "I know it will take a little getting used to, but I assure you, it will significantly improve your posture and strengthen the muscles around your spine."

Dimly, Lily wondered how she would tighten this garment on her own.

"You should wear it every day," the doctor added before handing her his business card and telling her to contact him if she ever wanted someone to show her around. "I know Darby can be difficult, but he's a good man, really. He just hasn't been the same since his wife, Naomi, passed."

Lily thanked him and he gave her one last dazzling

smile. "Welcome to Chateau Oriol. I hope you enjoy your stay."

3

When Lily went to lock her door, she realized there was no key. The keyhole stood empty where the large skeleton key Tomas carried in his pocket would fit. She'd have to ask him about that later. She didn't like the idea of leaving the door unlocked. Nor did she like the idea that Tomas had the only key.

But there was nothing she could do at the moment. She'd heard Tomas storm angrily down the hall.

She was tired, both from the long trip and the emotionally exhausting meeting with Mr. Darby, but Tomas had instructed her to change into her uniform and meet him in the kitchen right away.

Her uniform consisted of a simple black dress, black stockings with seams that ran up the backs of her legs, a ruffled white apron that tied around her cinched waist and black leather pumps.

The corset restricted her movements. Unable to bend at the waist, Lily was forced to pivot at her hips. Her stiff, unnatural movements made her think of a jewelry box ballerina.

She looked around the room for her suitcase to find it no longer where she'd left it, and when she went to the wardrobe, expecting to find her belongings stored away, she saw only a row of identical black dresses.

She slid her feet into the shoes provided for her. They were undoubtedly beautifully crafted, she'd felt it in the supple leather beneath her fingertips, but there was no way Mr. Darby could reasonably expect her to stand all day in heels this high. Looking around, Lily quickly realized they were the only shoes provided.

She checked the time and cursed again. Her appointment with the doctor had gone longer than she'd realized and she couldn't afford another reprimand on her first day.

With one last look at herself in the floor length mirror, she ran out the door.

The most delicious smells assailed her senses the moment she stepped into the kitchen. And what a kitchen it was. With marble counter tops and black and white tiled floors. The smell of meat roasting caused Lily's mouth to water and reminded her that she hadn't eaten since leaving Madrid early that morning.

It felt like a lifetime ago. The magnificent glass and steel train station like a greenhouse, filled with tropical plants and singing birds as she sipped a small, milky coffee, and waited for her train.

Her stomach growled loudly and Tomas shot her a withering look.

"You will eat in the kitchen once Mr. Darby has finished. Chef will show you which dishes to take out first.

Mr. Darby has an aperitif in his study before dinner." Tomas checked his watch before continuing. "He expects his drink served promptly at seven. Dinner is at eight, unless otherwise noted. Every morning, you will be given a schedule for the day."

She nodded, swaying slightly on her perilous heels. Her empty stomach paired with the restrictive corset made her light-headed and she gripped the counter, afraid that she might faint.

Suddenly, Lily understood the necessity of fainting couches.

But she did not have time to contemplate her predicament, for Tomas went to the cupboard and removed a crystal glass. "Three fingers of Scotch. Always in this glass."

He looked at her, waiting and she realized he expected her to pour the drink. With trembling hands, she poured the Scotch then watched as Tomas measured it against his rough, calloused fingers.

She held her breath until, begrudgingly, he gave her a nod of approval.

She took the drink and made her way towards the study where Mr. Darby waited.

Each step was torture. She walked slowly, careful not to slosh the amber liquid around in the glass. She could only imagine the harsh words Tomas would have for her if she spilled even a drop.

Sweat trickled down her spine. And then she was there, standing outside his study door. She closed her eyes, summoning her failing courage. She could do this. She'd worked as a waitress enough summers to know how to handle almost anyone.

But Mr. Darby wasn't just anyone. The men who frequented the local bar, while rough, were never as openly hostile as Mr. Darby during their brief first encounter.

With her head held high and the glass of whiskey carefully held in one hand, she opened the door to the study.

Early evening light filtered through the blinds, filling the room with a dusky glow and for the first time, she noticed the aroma of old books, and beneath it, the hint of cigarette smoke. Mr. Darby sat behind his desk, a phone pressed to his ear, his lips compressed in a thin line. He didn't so much as glance in her direction and she moved quietly, though her heels struck the carpeted floors, and placed the cloth napkin down in front of him and then his drink.

For a moment, she stood there, inches from him, torn between the desire to remain and the almost pressing need to flee.

Her heart pounded and she held her hands behind her back to stop them from trembling. Even in silence, the man was intimidating. She took short, quick breaths, all the corset would allow, and stared at his profile, noting his strong, masculine jaw. Something about his profile gave the impression of a picture slightly askew. She squinted, trying to determine what it was.

His nose, she realized at last. It looked as though, sometime long ago, it had been broken and not quite allowed to heal properly.

Rather than ruining his otherwise classically handsome features, this gave him an almost rugged appearance. As if, though surrounded by books, cut off from the rest of the world, he wasn't entirely above it. As if he were a man who understood physical labor.

Lily knew this was merely a flight of fancy. The man before her knew nothing of the toils of physical labor, of this she was certain.

Finally, after several tortured minutes, she turned to leave.

Mr. Darby grabbed her wrist and the surprise of this sudden contact caused Lily to lose her balance and stumble.

He slammed the receiver down and glared up at her. "Are you always so bloody clumsy?"

"I'm sorry," she apologized, though he was the one who had nearly knocked her off her feet.

He frowned as he took her in, examining her, and she held herself still. His eyes narrowed. "Your posture looks significantly improved."

"Thank you, sir."

"Charles informed me that I will be responsible for tightening the corset each morning. We will deal with it after my coffee."

She felt light-headed, dazed, and she wanted nothing more than a sip of water and to sit for a moment to catch her breath, but she nodded, showing that she had at least heard him.

"We may have to do something about your hair."

Without thinking, Lily patted her hair, tucked in a low bun at the nape of her neck. She had beautiful hair. Of that, she was certain. Beautiful long blond hair.

Her mother hated that about her. She always said she had hair like that before she got pregnant. But pregnancy had stolen away not only her freedom but also her once enviable looks. She'd say this glaring at Lily and Lily learned at an early age not to contradict her mother.

She had a wicked temper that she often directed at her only child. As if it was Lily's fault that she'd gotten pregnant at such a young age and that Lily's father had run off before Lily was even born.

"Take it down."

Keeping her eyes on the floor, Lily pulled the elastic from her hair, letting her blond locks fall around her shoulders.

She wanted nothing more than to run away.

Instead, she stood there, head tilted towards the ground, waiting for him to speak.

She flinched at the strike of a match.

Mr. Darby sighed heavily, filling the air with thick cigarette smoke. She expected some scathing remark, but he said nothing, smoking, and she knew he was watching her, searching for some reaction on her part, but she kept her face down, refusing to look at him, refusing to react.

"You may go."

It took all of her earthly willpower not to run from the room.

Dinner proved just as dreadful. Mr. Darby sat at the head of a long table, one man in a banquet hall that could easily accommodate twenty, and barely glanced at her. Candlelight illuminated the contours of his face and Lily couldn't help but wonder if he was lonely. Living here alone with only the staff. The isolation must have taken its toll.

The doctor had mentioned a wife, now deceased, and she wondered if that was the reason for his isolation. For seeing Mr. Darby at the table alone, she realized the depth of his solitude. And it frightened her. How could a man, who so obviously had means, choose a life such as this?

But it wasn't her job to consider such things. So she stood behind him and waited for his terse commands. Fetch me this. Get me that. Always in that sharp tone of voice that made her jump.

She poured him wine and then brought out his dinner. Her mouth watered at the sight and smell of his opulent feast. The standing rib roast, cooked to perfection, the meat tinged red, served with Yorkshire pudding and a rich Bordelaise sauce.

She was hungry. So hungry. But she waited patiently for him to finish so that she might go to the kitchen and eat her own meal, wondering if she'd be lucky enough to have the leftovers.

By the end of the night, Lily was so bone-weary, it took all she had just to remove the dreaded corset. She found a white nightgown on the bed and pulled it over her head before collapsing onto the bed.

She was too tired to remember to ask Tomas about the key to her bedroom door. Within seconds, she was asleep. She didn't dream.

.

4

A shrill ringing roused Lily. She sat up abruptly. The room was dark and still. For a few murky moments, she didn't know where she was. And then, in a rush, the memories returned. The chateau. The previous day. Mr. Darby. Her visit with the doctor.

When she looked at her watch, she saw it was five-thirty. She all but ran to the bathroom, locking the door behind her.

The bathroom, unlike her room, was spacious and well-appointed. She'd been too tired the night before to fully appreciate it. A deep claw foot tub sat in the middle of the room and she gazed at it with longing. One night, she'd take advantage of that bath. She'd soak in it for hours, until her skin puckered and wrinkled and it would be marvelous.

She washed her face and applied her makeup then returned to her bedroom and went about the difficult task of dressing. The corset with its long row of tiny eyelets. She dreaded the moment when Darby would tighten it for her, for even now it restricted her breathing.

She slipped her feet into the high heels, her arches aching, and made her way downstairs.

Tomas gave her a stern look but didn't say anything and she let out a sigh of relief. She'd done at least one thing right. She wasn't late.

Wordlessly, he handed her a schedule. It was written in clean, masculine writing that made her think it was Mr. Darby, and not Tomas, who had written it out the night before. Every second of the day was accounted for. There were even specified times allotted for using the restroom. Tomas had already explained she was never, under any circumstances, to use the bathrooms on the main floors, that she was expected instead to trudge upstairs.

At six-fifteen, Mr. Darby took coffee in the study along with the newspaper. Everything was already laid out on a polished silver serving tray, all Lily had to do was pick it up and bring it to the master of the house.

He sat at his desk, his posture rigid and his expression stern, though the sky was barely beginning to show signs of light. But as she made her way across the room, she realized how tired he looked. The bags beneath his eyes were dark and pronounced. She couldn't help but wonder if the lack of sleep had anything to do with his late wife.

For a moment, she pitied him. Living here in exile, as if he had committed a crime so heinous not even he could forgive himself. As if this magnificent house were not his home but his prison.

But when he glanced at her, all pity she felt dissolved. His dark brown eyes were cold and contemptuous. And she remembered, once again, that she was meant to be invisible. She placed the serving tray in front of him and stepped back nervously.

"Is there anything else?"

He stood wearily. "We must deal with your corset. Turn around and grip the table, it will help you keep your balance."

Lily blushed hotly when he lowered the zipper on her dress enough that her corseted torso was visible to him. She gripped the desk, and was not surprised to find that Mr. Darby yanked hard on the ties of the corset, knocking the air from her lungs. He tightened the corset roughly, with little concern for Lily's comfort, while Lily gritted her teeth to stop from protesting.

When he finished, he zipped up her dress and she heard his footsteps as he walked away.

She stood stiffly. "Sir?"

He didn't turn around and his voice was just as cold as it had been when they first met. "You may go."

So began Lily's life at Chateau Oriol. She served Mr. Darby with painstaking care, and he didn't so much as acknowledge her presence unless it was to criticize. No matter how hard she tried, it felt as though everything she did was wrong. But his words on her first day stuck with her, his expectation of failure. It gave her strength. She smiled through his insults, refusing to show they hurt. And she reminded herself that he was a grieving widower and that his anger, while directed at her, was really for the cruel world that had deprived him of his wife.

Whenever they were in a room together, she felt his eyes on her, like he was waiting for her to say something and then he'd almost smile, that slight twitch of his well-formed lips, and she knew she'd done at least one thing right. She'd kept her mouth shut.

Her duties, when not serving Mr. Darby directly, included keeping the extensive chateau in meticulous order. Dusting. Mopping. Laundering clothes. No job was considered beneath her. Each task was made more challenging by her tightly boned corset restricting her movements and the almost laughably high heels he insisted she wear. But Lily, accustomed to hard work, did not utter a word of complaint.

On her second day, she discovered the library. Its soaring ceilings and wood paneled bookshelves that reached two stories above her head. To Lily, it felt like stepping suddenly into a cathedral. Wooden ladders on rollers allowed her to reach even the books on the highest shelves. She knew she was to dust every inch of the room and dust she did, perched precariously on the ladder in her dangerously high heels, one hand gripping the smooth wood as she went about her task.

It took an entire afternoon. When she was finished, she stood back and contemplated the monumental room, feeling like Sisyphus. In the morning, she'd have to start again.

As she explored the long corridors of the chateau, shrouded in silence, she discovered many doors were locked, barring her entrance, including the door at the end of the second floor hallway that led to Mr. Darby's private quarters. But when she asked Tomas about it, he'd frowned and told her in that dissatisfied voice of his that doors had locks for a reason.

His response did nothing to stymie her curiosity.

Her first week passed quickly. She knew eventually she'd get accustomed to it, but by Sunday, her one day off of the week, she was too tired to ask Tomas to take her to the village. Too tired to do anything but lay in her narrow bed, staring at the ceiling and the thin crack that spread like a lifeline in the plaster. Or the veins on the underside of a maple leaf.

At least she had books. And so she spent her day off reading, excited by the knowledge that she could read any one of those books housed in the library downstairs. And when she tired of reading, she took a long bath, letting the hot water soothe her aching muscles. She even found on the vanity an expensive looking bottle of bubble bath. She used it sparingly, luxuriating in its rich aroma and the thick bubbles it produced.

5

Time moved differently at the chateau. The regimented schedule, the strange and often savage demeanor of her employer, the sneering looks from Tomas, it all compounded, threatening Lily with exhaustion. How would she possibly survive three long months here, with no one to talk to, no one to share in her miseries and the small delights of her days? The smell of the lavender, the cool mountain air, her breathtaking surroundings?

But there was no one. The chef refused to acknowledge her. Tomas did not try to hide his disdain. And Mr. Darby...Mr. Darby was too standoffish, distant and cold as he presided over his vast estate.

Lily stole rare moments for herself when she knew that no one would find her out, often sneaking out of the house and wandering the grounds, admiring the savage beauty of the isolated landscape. Wild blackberry brambles covered fences and threatened to choke out the other plants and Lily would pluck the ripe berries from their vines and plop them into her mouth.

Or else, in the library, she might take a moment to flip through a book. Mr. Darby had said nothing forbidding her from taking advantage of his vast library, though she knew that she would only be permitted such a luxury on her own time. But his extensive collection, ranging from fiction to botanical encyclopedias, thrilled her, and sometimes she couldn't resist the temptation.

One afternoon, after spending the entire morning dusting, amazed by how quickly the dust accumulated, Lily told herself she'd only sit for a moment, just to catch her breath, but she'd picked up *Jane Eyre*, and somehow, time had gotten away from her.

Her shoes lay on the floor at her feet where she'd kicked them off. The corset forced her to sit up straight, but she didn't mind, just as long as she was off her feet for a moment.

She didn't notice Darby steal into the library. It wasn't until he was standing directly in front of her, his arms crossed over his chest, a look of surprise on his face, that she realized she'd been discovered.

"I'm so sorry," she said, scrambling to her feet. "It won't happen again, I promise." Her mumbled apology only made him smile and cock his head as he looked down at her.

She slipped her feet into her shoes, thankful for the added height. For until this moment, she hadn't realized just how tall he really was.

"You read?"

His tone made Lily wonder if he was asking, in surprise, if she was capable of reading and she bristled with irritation.

"Of course I read!" she huffed, staring back at him

defiantly. For once, she didn't shrink away or lower her eyes to avoid his penetrating gaze. Both Mr. Darby and Tomas made it clear that they considered themselves better than her, but to think that she was illiterate…

They stared at each other for a long while and eventually, Mr. Darby chuckled, the first sign she'd seen since arriving at the chateau that he had any sense of humor at all.

He rubbed his jaw, drawing Lily's attention to the hint of stubble there. She hated him a little in that moment for having such a well-formed jaw.

"And what are you reading?"

His question caught her off-guard. It was the first time that he'd asked her anything personal at all. She glanced at the book she'd dropped onto the chair.

"*Jane Eyre*," she mumbled, certain he would disapprove as he seemed to disapprove of everything she did or said.

"A worthwhile book," he said, once more stroking his chin. His dark eyes shone with amusement, doing nothing to put Lily at ease. "I'll admit, I always preferred *Wuthering Heights*."

She brushed off her skirt before straightening her apron and saying, "I've never read it."

"You should."

To Lily's surprise, Darby turned and agilely climbed the wooden ladder. Without hesitating or even searching, he yanked a book from the shelf.

He crossed the room and held it out to her, an unexpected peace offering.

The leather-bound book showed signs of wear, as if it had been read and re-read many times before. She looked at Mr. Darby before taking it, certain there must be some catch. But his face showed no obvious signs of deception.

"Thank you."

He waved his hand dismissively. "If you're done, I'd like the fire lit in my office." With that, he wandered out of the library, leaving Lily to puzzle over his odd behavior.

She hugged the book to her chest for a moment before dropping it on the seat and scurrying after Mr. Darby.

That night, tucked in her narrow bed, Lily pressed her nose to the leather-bound book and inhaled deeply. The old book smell comforted her and she couldn't help but smile at the thought that perhaps, finally, Mr. Darby was warming to her.

How different it would be, living here, if Mr. Darby took a liking to her.

It was well past midnight when she forced herself to set the book aside and switch off the light.

She'd hoped, foolishly perhaps, that the book might give her some insight into her employer's mind.

She realized quickly, that if this book was any indication, she did not want to know any more.

If Lily expected Mr. Darby's behavior in the library to indicate a shift in his demeanor, she realized quickly her mistake. He treated her with the same bland disdain as always, though perhaps, she thought hopefully, he was just slightly less caustic in his remarks.

But she clung to the hope that brief kind encounter brought her. At times, as she scrubbed the floors or did the washing, she imagined Mr. Darby coming to her and asking about the book, eager for her thoughts. From there, their conversation would venture into more personal territory. He'd ask about her life back home and she'd tell him the truth. How lonely she had been. How worthless her mother made her feel. How she hoped, more than anything, not to end up like her, stuck in a small town, filled with seething resentments.

She yearned to bare her soul to him, receiving in return his compassion and his confidences. She wished to ask him about his late wife and why he still had her portrait hanging in the entry hall. Didn't it bring him sadness, seeing it there every day? It was easy to lose herself in this fantasy, hours spent recounting her life to a man who didn't exist, so that when the bell rang, she'd have to remind herself it wasn't real. That Mr. Darby, the real Mr. Darby, was nothing like the compassionate man she'd conjured in her head.

One afternoon, still lost in thought, preoccupied by imaginary conversations, she was surprised to see Tomas standing by the kitchen sink, his back turned to her. After her first few days, when he hovered over her, criticizing constantly, he'd finally relented, allowing her to work without his supervision.

It was not his presence in the kitchen that caused Lily to tremble, but what he was doing.

Water gushed from the faucet as he washed blood from his hands. Beside the door to the garden rested a rifle. Lily looked from the rifle to Tomas in horror.

His shirt was torn at the sleeve and caked in blood and dirt.

"What happened?" she asked when she was finally able to summon her voice.

Tomas slowly switched off the water and turned to face her, his mouth set in a grim line. There was blood smeared across his cheek and Lily backed away nervously.

"Boar," he grunted, wiping his wet hands on his thighs. "Be careful if you walk around the grounds. The boar aren't normally dangerous, but when they have their young...And there have been wolves seen in the area, though I haven't seen any personally." He shrugged his shoulders. "It's best to stay close to the house, especially after dusk. There's been a change to the schedule. Mr. Darby will take his afternoon coffee on the south terrace."

Lily took the tray from the table and left as quickly as she'd come, ruminating as she went over Tomas' warning. She had never considered herself to be in danger here until now.

But the south terrace was enough to make her forget her fears, at least momentarily. She loved it here and couldn't understand why Darby didn't spend more time here. From the flagstone terrace, she could look out on the breathtaking vistas of verdant mountains surrounding the estate. Here, she felt transported to some savage paradise.

It was there that she found Mr. Darby, basking in the afternoon sunshine, head back, eyes closed, a hint of a smile illuminating his handsome face.

He looked happy. Or if not happy, at least contented. And that made Lily smile. Until this moment, she hadn't realized how much his dark moods affected her own, and seeing that rare smile calmed her instantly.

She was too focused on his happy expression to notice the uneven paving stone. Her heel caught and she watched in horror as the tray flew from her hands and clattered noisily to the hard ground, the coffee cup shattering.

"You clumsy idiot!"

The shock of her fall momentarily paralyzed her. She shivered on the flagstone.

"I don't pay you to sit on your ass! Clean up that mess. Immediately!"

Lily scrambled to her feet, ignoring the pain shooting through her palms and scurried inside.

She needed several deep, calming breaths before she was able to return with a broom and dustpan. Dropping to her hands and knees, she began picking up the largest pieces of porcelain with her fingers, careful not to cut herself on their sharp edges as she placed them in the dustpan. All the while, Mr. Darby watched her in silence.

Tears pooled at the corners of her eyes and she pressed her lips together, trying to hold them back.

She would not cry. Not in front of him.

"Bring my coffee to the study so we can discuss this incident."

Lily nearly burst into tears as she fled into the house.

I will not cry, she told herself as she stood outside his office door, the coffee cup on its porcelain saucer balanced in her hands. I will not cry. And with that proclamation, she entered his office.

He stood by the window, his back to her as he waited for her to set his coffee down. Her hands trembled. She stared at her feet and waited.

He turned slowly. "I will not tolerate clumsiness," he said evenly.

"I'm sorry, sir. It won't happen again."

"Look at me."

Reluctantly, she lifted her face, looking Mr. Darby in the eyes.

He was uncommonly handsome. If only he smiled. If only he ever looked at her with anything but disdain.

Now was no different. But even in anger, his handsome

features were striking.

He stalked towards her. "What do you think we should do about this? Should I fire you? Should I deduct the cost of the cup from your pay? Would that teach you a lesson?" He picked up his metal cigarette case and carefully examined it while Lily took the deepest breath the corset allowed.

He extracted a cigarette and rolled it between his long fingers.

His silence terrified Lily more than his harsh words and she found herself saying, "Please don't fire me."

He lifted one eyebrow. "You've lasted longer than the previous girl," he said thoughtfully. "It would be a pity to have to find someone to replace you so late in the season. So tell me, what do you suggest? What punishment would best fit the crime?"

She stared at him, wishing she could go back in time. She would be more careful. She wouldn't fall and Mr. Darby would still be outside, basking in the sun as he took his afternoon coffee.

Lily squeezed her hands together and gasped as pain shot through her.

"You're injured."

Lily shook her head, "I'm fine, sir."

"Show me your hands."

Lily held them out, noticing now the bloody scrapes on her palms.

"That won't do." He sounded almost perplexed by his words and Lily looked up to find him frowning.

"We can revisit your punishment later. Sit down." When Lily didn't move, he motioned impatiently towards the desk. "I said, sit down."

Numbly, she obeyed, feeling ridiculous sitting on the edge of his large wooden desk, her heels not reaching the floor, holding her bloodied palms out in front of her.

He dropped his unlit cigarette and went in search of a first aid kit.

With surprising care, he washed her wounds with rubbing alcohol and cotton swabs while Lily chewed her lip to keep from making a sound.

She wasn't used to his kindness and somehow, seeing him bent over her hands, tending her wounds, confused her more than ever. If only he would just be cruel and she could continue hating him. But she realized in that moment that she did not hate him. Feared him, certainly, but she could not bring herself to hate him. Even now.

Carefully, he spread a thick salve across her palms before wrapping her hands in gauze and for a brief moment, she wondered why he kept such a complete first aid kit in his office.

"Doesn't it hurt?" he asked.

"Of course, sir."

"But you made no sound." His lips twitched in thought. "You either have an unusually high pain tolerance or else you're exceptionally stubborn." His dark eyes burned into her and for a moment, they simply stared at each other, as if seeing each other for the first time. "Which is it? A high pain tolerance or stubbornness?"

"A little of both, I think, sir," Lily responded truthfully. She had never considered herself to have a particularly high tolerance for pain. Nor had she ever considered herself uncommonly stubborn.

But the thought evaporated when he came to stand in front of her, so close she could smell him. She closed her eyes, too overwhelmed to look at him. He smelled of musky cologne, a hint spicy, a hint exotic. The result undeniably masculine, and for a moment, she let herself imagine it was someone else standing over her. Someone kinder. Someone who would press his lips to her palms, erasing her pain with his gentle compassion.

Shocked by the thought, her eyes flew open.

He watched her with a curious expression.

"Take the rest of the day off. I expect you in my office in the morning."

With that, he picked up his cigarette and Lily was dismissed.

Lily lay restless in her bed. She tried to read but found little respite in the tale of brutality and revenge.

Instead, she thought about the unexpected side of himself that Mr. Darby had shown her today. That brief glimmer of happiness on his face before she ruined it, shattering the calm just as she'd shattered the delicate porcelain cup.

And then, in his office, the way he'd handled her hands. Expertly. Tenderly. With such gentleness her skin still burned from his touch.

She often forgot that he'd once been married. That he wasn't always a cruel bachelor living in isolation. That there must have been a time when he had touched a woman regularly, with kindness and affection.

With love.

She dreaded whatever punishment the morning would bring, hoping that he would have mellowed overnight.

Yet, as much as she dreaded it, she ached to see him again. This realization confused Lily.

Her stomach rumbled, reminding her she hadn't eaten since morning. It was late. The house silent. She slipped from bed as quietly as possible, her bare feet on the cold floor, and made her way downstairs in the semi-darkness.

Shadows clung to the walls like ghosts. This house, which once must have overflowed with life, sighed and ached with solitude. The stairs creaked and groaned, every sound magnified by the still darkness. She reached for the kitchen door but froze, hand suspended in midair. Nervously she looked over her shoulder.

She saw only shadows.

She'd heard something.

She strained her ears, the darkness obliterating all her other senses, but she heard nothing but heavy, dampening silence. Silence that blanketed everything, making every breath she took sound deafening. Shaking her head, she continued to the kitchen. She must have imagined it. After all, Mr. Darby was surely in bed by now.

He always went to bed shortly after dinner. Though given how tired he looked most mornings, she doubted he did much sleeping once there.

And then she heard it again.

A moan. Like a wounded animal. A whimper.

Lily forgot her hunger. The sound came from the rear of the house. She followed it without thinking.

The cold stone against the soles of her feet was the only thing that made this feel real.

The moaning again, louder this time. What she'd at first thought had sounded like a wounded animal now sounded distinctly human. She hurried, her bare feet slapping the stone floor, her fear forgotten. What if he was hurt? Tomas was already locked away for the night in his carriage house. If something had happened, no one would hear his calls for help. No one but Lily.

She saw light at the end of the long corridor. The door, normally locked, was open a crack and light spilled across the floor.

She heard it again. The moan. It caused the hairs on her arms to stand up straight.

She stole forward, fear replaced by a burning curiosity.

Peering through the open crack, she saw Mr. Darby leaning against a table, his eyes closed, a cigarette burning between his fingers. Lily's lips fell open. Kneeling before him, with her hands clasped behind her, was a beautiful and naked woman. Her head moved up and down as she attended to Darby with only her mouth.

Mr. Darby moaned again. Not in pain, Lily realized, but in pleasure. He tightened his grip on the woman's chestnut mane, forcing her to take him deeper.

The woman struggled then stilled. The lean muscles of her back tensing with the exertion of holding her position. Darby lifted his cigarette to his lips and took a heavy drag.

Lily had never seen him so relaxed. Or vulnerable.

She knew she should leave. That this private moment was not meant for her eyes. But she couldn't bring herself to move. She told herself it was fear that held her in place but she didn't quite believe it.

When he let out one final growl, the hairs on the back of Lily's neck stood straight up. It wasn't the sound of a man she heard. It was the sound of a primal animal. Wild. Unrestrained. And terrifying.

For several beats, the woman remained kneeling at his feet, her head bowed, so Lily could see each vertebrae in her neck. The vulnerability of this position caused Lily to think of a beheading, a sacrificial lamb on the alter.

At last, Darby released his tight hold on her hair and she came gracefully to her feet. Lily admired her perfectly formed figure, the hourglass shape of her body, the swell of her hips and her naturally cinched waist.

"I was beginning to think you'd lost my number," she said in a melodic voice. "Don't tell me, your little girls aren't enough anymore?"

"Shut up, Brigitte," he snapped angrily.

"Edward!" she cooed with delight. "Don't tell me, she's different?"

He grabbed her roughly by the hair, forcing her back to her knees. "Enough!"

Her laughter filled the room, defiant laughter. Laughter that made Lily's body go cold. Even held down, the woman didn't seem the slightest bit afraid. In fact, she seemed to find the situation, and Darby's anger, amusing.

"Would you like to punish me?" she asked wickedly. "You could tie me up and put all that pent up rage to good use. I may be a little old for you these days, but I must say, some things get better with age."

With a look of disgust, he pushed her away and she came easily to her feet and leaned elegantly across the table for his cigarette case.

"You really should learn to control yourself better. This behavior is unbecoming." She waved her hand dismissively at Mr. Darby and then lit her cigarette, half-turning to face the door.

The woman squinted towards the darkened hallway and Lily pulled back, certain that they couldn't possibly see her, hidden as she was in shadows, but for a second, she thought she saw the woman give her a knowing smirk.

She turned back to Mr. Darby and said, "Tell me about her. Is she like the others? Plain? Innocent? Dull beyond compare?"

Lily backed away then turned and fled, running up the main staircase though she knew if anyone found out, she'd be severely reprimanded.

Once in her room, she shut the door, wishing that she could lock it and then crawled under the blankets.

Lily knew she was inexperienced. She let a boy kiss her on the mouth once, but he was drunk and the stench of beer on his breath made her queasy. When she pushed him away, he spat on the ground at her feet before wandering off to find someone more amenable.

Lily had no words for what she'd seen. It terrified her. At first, she'd been scared for the woman, seeing the rough way that Mr. Darby treated her, but then, when she was standing, facing off with him, Lily realized she was no longer scared for the woman.

She was scared of her.

Lily trembled and pulled her blankets up, hoping for warmth that she knew would not come. What she'd seen...it had sparked something inside of her. Some feeling she couldn't identify. Some want she couldn't admit.

Without thinking, she slipped her trembling hand beneath her nightgown, pushing the thin fabric up around her waist. She stroked herself through her underwear, wondering what it would feel like to kneel before a man, before Mr. Darby. Because the truth was, Mr. Darby, despite his cold, uncompromising demeanor, had worked his way into her heart.

Lily wondered what it tasted like. What *he* tasted like.

She'd overheard girls laughing in the bathroom at school about it one afternoon as Lily hid in the stall, waiting for them to leave. It's vile, but just breathe through your nose and you'll survive, one girl had said haughtily. It's not like you *have* to swallow.

Her tone made Lily think it wasn't really a choice.

It surprised Lily to find that her underwear were moist. She wiggled them off then pressed her fingers to her sex. Her cold fingers on her burning flesh. She closed her eyes, exploring tentatively. What would it feel like, if someone else were touching her? Making love to her body with their hands, strong masculine hands with the long, elegant fingers of a pianist.

He had magnificent hands.

She felt the slick arousal on her fingers, surprised and when she brushed her clit, she jumped.

It felt electric. A live wire to her skin when before, the pleasure of her touch was always muted.

She clamped one hand over her mouth to muffle her moans. Every sound in this house echoed. Every creak of the bed was deafening.

She rolled her head to the side and stared hard at the door as she stroked herself, once more wishing she had the key.

But what did it matter? Mr. Darby was downstairs and Tomas was gone for the night. She was alone. No one could hear her. She could do as she pleased.

She slid two fingers into her sex, moving them in and out as she imagined a man would do if he were fucking her. Is this what it would feel like? To finally have sex?

Shuddering at the exquisite pleasure, Lily moaned softly then froze.

She'd heard something. A sound. Her fingers buried in her sex. She looked around, but in the shadowy darkness, there was nothing to see.

Her chest rose and fell erratically.

It must have been the wind ripping through the trees outside her tiny bedroom window.

But even as her breathing returned slowly to normal, the moment was lost. Sighing heavily, Lily rolled onto her side and tried to sleep. But she could not get the image out of her head. It replayed over and over again. Only this time, instead of standing outside the door, Lily imagined herself in the room.

On her knees.

She imagined herself in the position of the woman.

And that other woman gone.

Lily would never admit it but she wasn't just afraid of that woman.

She was jealous.

6

The kitchen was cold when Lily arrived in the morning, ready to take Mr. Darby his coffee. But there was no coffee prepared, no newspaper folded on the tray. And then she saw the note. Sitting on the kitchen table where her schedule usually was.

She picked it up, expecting the worst. That Mr. Darby had somehow discovered her last night. That she was being dismissed.

I have gone away for a few days. I'm not certain when I will return. You may take today off. I expect the house to be in perfect condition when I return. -D

That was all. Lily's heart thudded, and she wondered if the woman last night, Brigitte, had seen her standing in the doorway. And who was she? Brigitte. Even the name sounded exotic in Lily's mind. So unlike her own plain name.

Lily felt disappoint welling up inside of her when what she should have felt was excitement. A day off. She could rest. She could go to town. But with whom? She was alone. She knew no one. Except the doctor, but she felt strange just thinking about contacting him, though he'd been perfectly nice when he'd extended the offer and Lily knew he was being genuine. But he had also seen her at her most vulnerable, naked except for a cloth gown, stretched out on the exam table. She blushed, remembering the horrible exam. How could she sit and have coffee with him now?

She looked down at her uniform and shook her head. She couldn't go to town dressed as she was. She'd have to find Tomas and ask for her clothing back. Surely, Mr. Darby wouldn't begrudge her that.

She thought, perhaps, she'd imagined the night before.

With Mr. Darby gone, time moved sluggishly forward. The house was still. Silent. Eerie. Tomas appeared and disappeared like a shadow, always when she least expected him.

To Lily's surprise, she found she missed Mr. Darby. She told herself that it was because he was the only person here with whom she ever spoke. Though they rarely exchanged more than a few words at a time. Without him, the solitude and isolation of the great house bore down on her like a heavy, inescapable weight.

Every day was the same. Monotonous. Tedious. Without Mr. Darby, she was left to amuse herself. She dusted the library. She read in the comfortable chair where Mr. Darby had discovered her that one day before presenting her with *Wuthering Heights*.

She scrubbed the floors. She cleaned every room except those that were locked. She wondered what lay behind those locked doors, and pressed her eye to the keyholes, but she saw only darkness.

When she heard the gravel in front of the house kicked up under the wheels of a car, Lily straightened with excitement. Then the angry slam of a door. And then the shrill bell ringing, loudly, and she tucked her duster into her apron and walked as quickly as she could, her heels echoing on the tile floor.

Mr. Darby stood in front hall, dressed as usual in a pale colored oxford, his hair looking uncommonly mussed, and when she stopped in front of him, she thought, for a second, that she saw just a trace of a smile.

As if he were pleased to see her.

The thought made her giddy.

"Bring me a drink," he said before storming off towards his office, erasing whatever giddiness she might have felt a second before. "And light a fire! It's bloody freezing!"

She hurried after him excitedly and knelt before the fireplace, stacking the wood carefully before lighting it with a long match. The kindling caught quickly.

She loved the smell of the fire burning. For once, it lent the house a homey feel.

She stood awkwardly, brushing her hands on her apron, and went to the bar to pour his usual whiskey. Three fingers. No ice.

He stood at the window, watching her intently. She handed him the drink and before she could think better of it, she asked about his trip.

For a tense moment, he looked astounded, no doubt by her overly familiar question, and then, in a low voice that Lily felt vibrate through her body, he said, "It was necessary."

His answer surprised her.

"Was it a business trip?" she inquired, unable to hide her curiosity. For days, she had had no one to speak to and her voice felt tight and rusty in her throat.

He shook his head. "No, it was not a business trip." His terse response did not encourage further discussion and Lily bowed her head.

"Is there anything else, sir?"

She held her breath, hoping for something. An excuse to spend a few more minutes in his presence.

"No, that will be all for now."

She couldn't hide her disappointment and turned to leave, wishing that for once, just once, he would treat her as an equal. Someone with whom he could talk. Someone with whom she could talk.

She didn't realize, until this moment, just how much she missed having someone to speak to. How hard it was to spend so many hours in silence, with only her thoughts to keep her company.

Just as she'd placed her hand on the door handle, he spoke. "Stop."

She froze.

"Turn around."

Slowly, she turned, her heart thundering in her chest. "Sir?"

For a moment, he just stared at her and she felt her pulse quicken. "I have guests coming this weekend. I expect you to be on your best behavior."

His words stung. "Have I done something wrong?" she asked softly.

He stared at her and she felt the color come to her cheeks. Finally he shook his head. "Close the door on your way out."

His words hurt worse than a reprimand and she hurried out of his office, fearing that she might start crying if she didn't get away from him fast enough.

That night, in bed, she did cry. She hugged her pillow to her chest and wept. She didn't understand why she wept, only that she couldn't stop the tears. And once they started, it felt as if they would tear her apart.

The guests arrived in fancy cars as Lily watched from a window on the second floor. Beautiful men and women dressed in elegant evening attire that seemed so out of place in the country and yet, so appropriate in a house such as this.

In total, they were six. Plus Mr. Darby. Lily could not believe the relief she felt when she realized Brigitte was not among them.

They were seated in the grand library, the fire that Lily had lit before they arrived burning brightly, filling the room with a comfortable warmth. For though it was summer, the thick stone walls of the chateau kept the interior cool.

She rolled in a heavily stocked bar cart and served drinks. The ladies drank pink champagne from crystal flutes. The men, whiskey. A victrola filled the lofty room with baroque classical music.

His guests didn't so much as look at her when they held out their hands, waiting for their glasses to be refilled. Once more, she was invisible. And all she wanted was to be seen. She envied the women their beautiful evening gowns. She envied the attention of the attractive men. For they were all attractive, though none held her attention in the way that Mr. Darby did. While obviously all rich, they lacked his understated regal bearings. The way he held himself as if the world belonged to him and him alone.

Mr. Darby looked at her. She felt his eyes on her, studying her. She yearned for a kind word, but when he addressed her, it was only to demand she refill a glass or poke the fire. She found herself often on her knees, making sure the logs burned brightly.

There were times, alone in her room, when she looked at herself in the floor length mirror and thought her maid's uniform elegant. Now, she realized how foolish that thought was. Next to the dresses worn by these women, it was obvious it was nothing. She stood against the wall of books, her hands clasped in front of her, until one of them called to her. Small and invisible.

A man like Mr. Darby would never notice someone like her. She was too plain. Too ordinary. The only thing special about her was her long blond hair, but she wore it in a bun at the nape of her neck so that it didn't get in her way.

These women, they were extraordinary. Perfect in every conceivable way. Their skin was like porcelain and it glowed, in health and wealth. Even their voices were perfect, melodic, rich.

They moved with the slow ease of people who had never had to hurry. Who'd never had to work a day in their lives.

The voluptuous blond motioned to her and she hurried over. She kept her eyes down, focusing on the emerald hanging from a black velvet choker around her neck.

"What are you called?" the woman asked, her voice dropping.

"Lily."

The woman smiled and for a moment, just a moment, Lily felt alive.

"How sweet," she said, turning back to Mr. Darby. "Where *do* you find these girls?"

He gave her a tight-lipped smile and Lily felt the color come to her cheeks. They burned and she wished she could leave, that he would let her free for the night, but she knew he wouldn't dismiss her until dinner was through.

She feared the night would go much longer.

Luckily, the woman seemed to lose interest in Lily and she was able to slip back into a corner and hide, invisible in plain sight.

But while invisible, she wasn't deaf. And Lily listened to their conversations, breathless with envy. They spoke of art and travels and politics. They spoke with knowledge and grace and Lily once more found herself envious. For they lived in a world where such things were not a privilege, but a right, and it was amazing to behold, knowing that this world was one that would never open its doors for her.

Lily glanced at her wrist and realized it was nearly time for dinner and the chef would be displeased if she seated them late. She cleared her throat and the talk around her ceased as everyone in the room turned to look at her with bland interest.

She blushed.

"Dinner will be served in fifteen minutes. Is there anything else I can provide?"

Mr. Darby stared at her, and she could feel the color come to her cheeks. Something in his eyes was different tonight. Something in his expression, like he wanted to say something. Instead, he dismissed her with a shake of his head.

Outside, she sucked in a deep breath. She was so accustomed to being alone with Mr. Darby that she'd forgotten what it was like seeing other people.

She didn't have time to over-think it. She scurried off to the kitchen to make sure everything was perfect for the first course.

Dinner went off without a hitch. She served them then stood aside and watched them eat, her mouth watering at the delicious smells that filled the magnificent dining room. The first course was a chilled asparagus soup. The second course, venison. Lily had never tried venison before, but the smell that wafted from their plates made her reconsider her thoughts on eating deer, an animal she had always considered too helpless and beautiful to eat. She hoped there would be leftovers so she could try at least a bite.

She watched them with growing envy. What would it be like, to live this way? The women pushed food around their plates and Lily watched in disgust, swearing if she was ever in their position, she wouldn't waste a single morsel.

She'd eat everything with relish, savoring each delicious, rich, marvelous bite.

The chef hadn't spared a single expense on the dinner. The venison plates were removed, replaced with a bountiful cheese platter that Lily set in the middle of the table. Rich brie spilled from its rind. Blue cheese, pungent and creamy, sat beside it. Grapes spilled from the plate. And cherries like Lily had never seen before, white with a hint of a blush.

She watched the voluptuous blond pluck a cherry from the platter with her perfectly manicured nails and plop it into her lush mouth.

Lily watched her chew with growing hatred.

It felt like ages before Mr. Darby snapped his fingers and she went to fetch the final course.

The chocolate soufflé towered out of its ceramic mold and Lily took tiny steps, afraid that if she walked unevenly, the aerated confection would fall and she would face the wrath of not just Mr. Darby, but also chef, who had looked at her sternly before relinquishing the dessert.

Tiny porcelain plates were passed around the table. And Lily served each guest a portion of the soufflé, the rich chocolately aroma filling the air, making her stomach grumble.

What she wouldn't do for just one bite. To lick the silver serving spoon.

Instead, she watched them eat. Like decadent gluttons. The men filling their bellies. The women laughing cruelly, their painted lips, the champagne in their glasses always needing to be refilled.

As they drank more and more, their laughter grew louder.

When all that remained of the soufflé were smears of chocolate on their plates, Mr. Darby stood. He brushed the crumbs from his lap and tossed his napkin on the table.

"Shall we move to the Game Room?"

The meal that had felt interminable was finally over. Mr. Darby didn't bother to look at Lily before he led the way down the hall and she could hear him unlock the door at the end of the hall, the same room where she'd caught him with Brigitte.

The Game Room.

The blond glanced at her before asking in that musical lilt of hers, "Is she joining us?"

Lily froze, waiting for his response, secretly dying to know what lay beyond that locked door. She stared at Mr. Darby expectantly and he met her level gaze as he said firmly, "No."

His tone left no room for argument. With laughter, they retired behind the door at the end of the hall and she heard it lock behind them. She wished to know what happened behind those closed doors. Wished to be a part of their beautiful, sophisticated evening.

She cleared the table. And alone in the kitchen, she took a spoon and ate the remains of the soufflé from the dish, scraping the leftovers onto the spoon and feeling the rich dessert dissolve on her tongue.

7

Lily stared at the door that stood between her and the Game Room, where she'd watched Mr. Darby and his guests disappear the evening before. She imagined the women reclining languidly on opulent sofas, surrounded by the handsome men.

She pressed her eye to the keyhole but could see nothing but shadows beyond and she stepped back in disappointment.

Why did he insist on so many locked doors? So many places she wasn't permitted? The one time she'd asked if he would like her to clean his bedroom, he'd stared at her as if he hadn't understood the question before quickly dismissing the idea.

She lifted her hand to the doorknob, glancing over her shoulder, before turning it, just to see.

She was surprised to feel the knob turn easily in her hand. He'd be livid if he found her in here, but he'd left early that morning, telling her only that he would return later. She'd watched from the front steps as Tomas slipped behind the wheel of the car and drove off.

What could be the harm? Just a peek. And then she'd leave. No one would know. She'd be in and out long before Mr. Darby and Tomas returned.

With one final glance over her shoulder, she opened the door and slid inside.

She blinked in the dimly lit room. Shadows abounded. The curtains were drawn so only a thin sliver of light cut through the darkness and Lily felt the wall for the light switch.

The aroma of leather and cigarettes hung in the air but nothing prepared Lily for the sight before her.

She took a step back, backing into the door with a loud bang and she let out a low curse and stilled. If anyone found her in here, she'd be punished. Severely. If she'd had any doubts before, she knew that certainly now.

For she was standing in an elegantly appointed torture chamber. How else could she describe it? The walls were papered with red damask wallpaper and she knew, if she ran her hands along them, she'd feel the raised patterns in velvet. The room was peppered with almost dainty Louis XV furniture, all elegant, all exquisite.

In front of her was a large leather and wood cross, from which hung leather chains and shackles. Her mouth fell open. Everywhere she looked, shackles. They hung from the ceiling, from the walls.

Yes, a room for torture, but yet, also for pleasure, she surmised. The gold settee before her looked worn and comfortable, the indentations left in the pillows hinting at many hours spent sitting there.

She recognized it from the portrait hanging in the front hall. And she shivered, imagining that beautiful woman here. Naomi Darby.

What had happened here while Lily was left to scrub dishes in the kitchen?

Suddenly she understood why Mr. Darby kept this door locked. This, she realized, was the part of him that he wanted to keep hidden. Not just from her, but from the public at large.

Beside a fireplace filled with ash hung various whips. Lily had to fight the urge to clean the fireplace out, knowing that if she did, Darby would know that she'd been here. But she'd spent enough time in the chateau that cleaning felt like second nature to her. If she saw a smudge, she was compelled to wipe it away.

She took a step forward and then another and before she knew it, she was running her fingers along one of the long leather whips, feeling the tails so soft against her hand.

What happened here? she wondered, her heart pounding, her mouth dry. What unspeakable tortures? And yet, she felt also a strange yearning. One that made her pull her hand back as if the leather burned her skin.

For despite her innocence, Lily knew the truth. That though these devices she saw before her could be used for torture, they had an air of sensuality to them. She remembered the naked woman kneeling before Darby, the image in her mind causing her to blush with embarrassment.

She knew she should leave immediately, that at any moment Darby might return and catch her here. The thought, though terrifying, excited her. She wanted to understand, wanted to learn more about her capricious master.

She did not hear the door open. Her eyes continued to rove every darkened corner. For the more she looked, the more she saw.

"What the hell are you doing?"

Lily jumped. She could sense Darby's anger before she even turned to face him, letting her eyes fall to the ground in a silent symbol of servility.

"I'm sorry, sir. I'll go," she whispered, though a part of her wished to remain, to satisfy her curiosity.

She made her way towards the door, but he grabbed her wrist, stopping her in her tracks. She felt his touch as if it were an iron, branding her.

"I've been too lax. I've let things slide that I would never have allowed with one of the girls before you. That stops now." Something about his cold tone that made Lily pull back, but his grip on her wrist only tightened, his fingers bruising her delicate skin.

"Sir?"

"Dalton explained your condition and I foolishly allowed it to color my judgment. I will not tolerate snooping."

The color drained from her cheeks. She'd never heard him so cold before. For the first time since arriving at Chateau Oriol, Lily was truly afraid.

"Sir?" she squeaked.

"Quiet. I need to think." He rubbed his temples as if he had a headache.

She swallowed hard.

"I keep this door locked, do I not?"

She nodded.

"And why do you think that is?"

"So no one comes in?"

"Precisely. I lock this door because I want to keep people out of this room. And knowing that, knowing that this room is off-limits, you decided to enter it. Am I correct?"

She gave a resigned nod and whispered, "Yes, sir."

"Better. I think it's time you learn your place. You are here to serve me. And you've done a mediocre job at that. I've tolerated it, but this—" he waved his hand at the room before them, "—this is unacceptable."

"Don't fire me." Her eyes widened in panic.

He laughed. A cruel laugh that made the hairs on the back of her neck stand up straight. "Girl, when I'm done with you, you will wish I'd fired you."

With that, he dropped her wrist and walked away. She shivered, watching him lift the same whip just moments before she'd been stroking, idly imagining what it would feel like against her skin.

Now, she hoped never to know the answer.

She watched his careful deliberation, the way he lifted and weighed each whip and crop. Her heart thudded in her chest and she struggled to breathe in the restrictive corset that bound her.

Finally, he took down several and placed them on the low table in the middle of the room. When he looked at her, he must have seen the fear radiating from her face because he said quietly, "I see you're beginning to understand your predicament."

She swallowed hard and nodded her head, her eyes returning to the terrible items on the table. He couldn't possibly mean to...

"Sir?"

He tapped his fingers impatiently on the table. "Would

you like to pick or shall I?"

Was that amusement she heard? She wondered, for the first time, if perhaps he was enjoying himself. And the significance of such a fact.

When she didn't respond, he frowned and she hated seeing that frown on his beautiful face. And all that it might mean.

"This isn't for your enjoyment, though I wonder if you might enjoy it even so. Now, decide. Or I will."

Her mind raced as she glanced between the various instruments of torture before her. She had no basis of comparison, no way of knowing if the small riding crop would cause more pain than the large flat paddle or the soft suede tails of the whip.

"Sir, I can't…"

"I hoped you might say that." The smile he gave her made Lily's blood run cold.

She was trapped. Not by actual bonds but by the knowledge that trying to escape would only postpone the inevitable. She had nowhere to go, and Mr. Darby, in his unhurried movements, seemed to realize that.

He lowered himself onto the faded settee and patted his thigh.

Head hanging in shame, she approached, and then, when she was standing beside him, he pulled her down onto his lap, her torso pressed against his muscular thighs, her hair spilling to the floor.

She didn't anticipate the first blow of his hand against her ass and she screamed as much from surprise as from the sting.

"Count each blow. If you lose count, or stop, we will begin again. Understood?"

"Yes, sir."

She hadn't been spanked since she was a child, and even then, it happened only infrequently. When her mother was truly upset. Lily had learned quickly not to upset her mother. Not to make a sound when she had visitors. She would hide in her room, with a flashlight, under the sheets and read, trying to ignore the sounds emanating from the living room.

Moans.

Pants.

Cries.

She'd hated every second of it, the shame it caused her, the fear, but she'd pushed it aside, forgetting all about it until this moment. Until she found herself draped over Mr. Darby's lap, her ass in the air, as he delivered blow after blow and she sobbed into the musty settee.

She struggled to keep track, as she counted out each blow in a voice that wavered. Her ass radiated heat, like it was on fire. Not even when her mother was most angry did she spank Lily with such brutal force.

She sobbed loudly when she reached twenty. And when he began massaging her ass, she felt relief, thinking her torture finished. But it was not over. He pushed up her skirt roughly. She struggled, writhing against him, but he held her pinned tightly to his lap. She felt something stir beneath her, pushing insistently against her belly, and it sent a chill down her spine.

He was enjoying this.

When he peeled down her tights, leaving them bunched around her thighs, keeping her legs pinned together and then yanked down her panties, her sobs intensified. She felt only shame. And terror. No one had seen her so undressed before, except the doctor, and he had been so kind. So friendly.

He had treated her with respect. Or so she had thought.

There was no respect in the way Mr. Darby manhandled her. There was only power.

"You pinken quite nicely," he said thoughtfully. "But I think we could do a little better, don't you?"

She sobbed. He laughed. He hoisted her off his lap, depositing her on her feet beside him. She kept her eyes to the floor, her hair curtaining her tear-stained face. She wept in silent shame.

He stood, pushing her aside, making her feel suddenly small and weak. Her panties hung between her thighs awkwardly and her skirt was still pushed around her waist. She felt so naked. So very naked.

She felt violated.

He did not give her time to consider her situation. "Kneel and lean over the table."

Awkwardly, she did as he commanded, hoping only that he would stop his torture.

He leaned his long, hard body over her, reaching for the many-tailed whip.

"This is a flogger."

She felt the suede tails trail along her naked behind, making her quiver. The feeling, much to her surprise, was not unpleasant. And yet, that odd comfort that it gave her made her fear it all the more. She tried to recoil but she was trapped between Mr. Darby and the table.

"Yes, you are right to be afraid."

She sobbed silently.

"Count."

"Yes, sir."

He hit her hard. Mercilessly. He rained blows down on her ass. She felt like she was on fire. Her skin burned. Not only with pain, but from the heat radiating from her skin. From the shame and humiliation of being so exposed before the man she'd secretly admired.

A man she had thought cold because of his loss. Because of his inner, secret pain.

Now, she realized, he was just cold. Hard. Brutal.

This was the true Edward Darby. A man who delighted in causing her pain.

She tried to ignore the dull throbbing heat between her legs, but like her pain, it was impossible to ignore.

She heard the flogger drop to the ground and she sobbed with relief, resting her cheek against the cool wood of the table, now wet with her tears. Her torture finally over. And then she felt his hands, so large, so imposing, against her burning flesh. She jumped at the contact, her inner muscles contracting uselessly.

"Your ass is surprisingly pleasant to look at," he said and she couldn't tell if she was meant to be relieved at this comment or further afraid.

She almost expected him to reach down and touch the throbbing place between her legs. And there was some part of her brain, foggy, confused, uncertain, that might even have craved that touch.

Instead, his hands dropped away and he sat back, and she imagined him surveying his work.

She burned.

She heard the flick of a lighter then smelled the cigarette smoke. She did not move, desperately fighting the urge to pull down her skirt and cover her nakedness.

She did not know how long he kept her on her knees. But every second felt like forever and she was thankful only to have the table to rest against because she did not know if she could hold herself upright.

And just as much as she craved to be alone in this moment, to lick her wounds in private, she also craved the sound of his voice. To know that he had not forgotten her.

She squeezed her eyes shut and prayed that this was all a terrible nightmare, that she would wake in her uncomfortable little bed, alone, cold, but unharmed.

He cleared his throat. "Clean yourself up," he said, his voice devoid of any emotion that might give her a clue into what he was thinking. "I'll take my coffee on the south veranda."

He stood, patting her ass one final time and she cringed, the light touch reigniting her pain.

Only when she heard the door open and close again did she finally stand, shakily, and pull her panties up, her tights back in place and her skirt down. She brushed the tears from her eyes. For a moment, she stood still and felt the way her body hummed with excitement. And then she scurried out of the room, wishing she had never entered it, wishing she had never decided to check the doorknob, knowing that if she didn't get his coffee quickly, he would have another reason to punish her.

When she passed Tomas in the hall, he smiled at her knowingly and she felt her face turn a deeper shade of red. For in that instant, she realized he knew exactly what Mr. Darby had done to her. That knowledge shone on his face.

She scurried away, her shame complete.

With trembling hands, she brought Mr. Darby his coffee. He was sitting on the veranda, the sunshine illuminating his placid expression. He looked so calm, so composed. She expected him to say something, to address what had just happened. But he said nothing, dismissing her with a wave of his hand.

That night, she felt the throbbing between her legs, the unmistakable arousal on her thighs compounding her shame. When she had arrived in her room, exhausted, drained, broken, she'd found a glass jar of lotion on the bed and a note in Darby's clear, masculine hand instructing her to use it on her bruised and beaten skin.

This sudden kindness illuminated the cruelty of earlier. She could no longer pretend that what had happened had been an invention on her part. That lotion, so beautiful in its glass jar, made everything real.

And when she untwisted the cap, the smell of rose petals filled her nostrils, a smell so rich and beautiful she nearly cried.

At first, it stung as it seeped into her wounds and then, a sense of warmth and comfort soothed her pain.

That night, she tossed and turned. The rough sheets felt harsh against her abraded flesh, keeping her awake. She replayed the afternoon again and again, unable to truly comprehend that it was real.

Unable to sleep, she reached between her thighs and pleasured herself, weeping when she came, disgusted with herself and the need that Darby's cruel treatment had awakened in her.

PART TWO

8

Darby called it the Game Room and the door was no longer kept locked after that afternoon. The following morning, as Lily stood before his desk, having served him his coffee and newspaper, he checked his wristwatch quickly. "I expect you in the Game Room at nine o'clock sharp so we may continue your training."

Training. She shivered with fear, remembering the cruel blows he'd delivered to her exposed backside and turned an even brighter shade of crimson when she thought about the wet heat between her thighs that resulted.

At nine on the dot, she found Mr. Darby sitting on the gold settee, one leg crossed over the other, his ankle resting on his knee, his manner relaxed.

"You may shut the door," he said and she turned and did as he told her, hearing the door click shut. She flinched, for now they were alone. With a heavy heart, she turned, keeping her eyes on the ground and her hands clasped before her.

"I've never understood the fascination some men have

with virgins," he began, causing Lily to blush. "It's always seemed so tedious, though I suppose I can see the appeal of knowing you alone have explored the untouched flesh. Still, it seems so exhausting, so…" he paused, searching for the correct word and drawing a blank, continued anyway, "There are obviously other recourses in a situation such as this. I could hand you over to be trained, or else, I'm sure I could make a pretty penny offering you to the highest bidder. Someone would be interested in taking you on."

Lily's eyes snapped up as his words sunk in. He let her panic, enjoying the way her eyes widened before he continued, "Lucky for you, I'm not interested in money." He waved one hand in front of him, as if to encompass all that he already owned. And it was true. What could he possibly do with more money than he already had? "It's a messy business, in any case, and not one I'm particularly fond of."

Lily breathed out a sigh of relief but could not shake the sensation that the other shoe had yet to drop.

He smiled, as if amused by her reaction. It was the smile of a cruel predator. The smile of someone who knew he had already won. When Mr. Darby stood, Lily took a step back, trying to maintain the distance between them, knowing in her soul that it was useless.

Her eyes dropped to the floor.

When he ran his finger along her cheek, she jumped and he chuckled at her response.

"So skittish. Like a doe," he said thoughtfully as he circled her, examining her like a rare artifact.

It was a struggle to remain still. A struggle not to run for the door. And yet, somehow, she managed it.

"Undress," he said at last and she looked up, eyes wide.

"Please, don't make me do this," she begged. Begged with her words and with her eyes but he considered her without compassion.

"Undress or I will undress you myself which I assure you will be far less pleasant."

Her breasts pushed against the tightly boned corset with each ragged breath she took. When it was clear he would not relent, Lily began to strip. Her dress fell to the ground and she stood before him in her panties and stockings, her heels and her corset, and quivered, hoping he would not ask for more and yet, knowing that he would.

He snapped his fingers, making her jump. "Everything."

She could not disobey him any more than she could run from this room.

She slipped her feet from her high heels, feeling the carpet beneath her toes and then, slowly, burning with shame, she eased down her stockings. She undid the corset with some difficulty, her fingers struggling with the tiny metal fastenings.

Finally, she stood in the middle of the room, completely naked as Mr. Darby examined her, humming to himself. Lily recognized the tune but could not place it.

"He was quite right," he said finally. "Charles has a knack. It's infuriating. But your skin takes color nicely. And the corset has certainly improved your posture. You are not unappealing on the eyes. Of course, your breasts are rather small, but they are nicely shaped. I've always been a proponent of quality over quantity."

She blushed horribly, feeling no better than a piece of

meat at the butcher's. Knowing he enjoyed the marks he'd left upon her body the night before terrified her. She'd twisted to see herself in the bathroom mirror. The hand prints. The lashes from the flogger. Her skin, normally so pale, an angry red.

He cupped her breast, his cool palm causing her nipple to instantly harden. Her shame complete. Finally, he released her breast and nudged her foot with the tip of his shoe. "Spread your legs, shoulder width apart and bend over, grasping your ankles."

Shame washed over her as she complied. Thus positioned, she was helpless. Helpless and exposed. She knew, despite her fear, despite her terror, that her pussy, hidden behind its thatch of blond hair, was beginning to moisten and such a detail would not escape his watchful gaze.

She could hide nothing from him now.

She expected his touch. Waited for it, breath held. Waited but it never came. Instead, she heard the cigarette lighter snap shut and smelled the smoke.

"You are too sore today to punish properly. Better to let you heal. But you shall stay in this position until I tell you otherwise."

She flinched when he patted her behind. She heard him move away and swiveled her head, trying to follow his movements with her ears. But the carpet muffled his steps and for all she knew, he stood directly behind her as he peered at her most intimate parts.

The thought made her stomach twist.

The thought made her wet.

She sobbed noiselessly as he watched, no doubt amused by her suffering. He was a cruel, cruel man, she realized in horror. And she was his captive. His prisoner. She thought of her passport, locked away in the safe in his office, for "safekeeping," he'd said. She realized now the truth. She could go nowhere. Had nowhere to go.

She could fight him, but he would win. She could cry, but he would only enjoy her sobs. Resigned, she endeavored to cry as proudly as a person could cry. For she didn't want him to enjoy the depth of her misery.

What she did not realize was, this struggle he was witnessing, was exactly what he enjoyed most.

The way her pride fought against her desire. The way her body and mind toiled. But with her head between her legs, she saw none of that. Blood rushed to her head, making her dizzy and she swayed, suddenly afraid she might stumble and fall and the punishment she'd no doubt receive as a result. Her muscles fought her. Her body ached. But she did not protest. Her tears fell, but she would make no sound.

He watched, enjoying every second of it.

When he finally told her that she could stand, she did so stiffly, refusing to meet his gaze.

She reached for her dress, hanging from the back of a chair and he slapped her wrist lightly.

"No. You will spend the rest of the day as you are. You have not earned the right to be clothed."

Only then did she look at him, her pink lips parted in a silent plea, her cheeks flushed, and he laughed.

"Run along, now." He glanced at his watch. "It's time for my lunch. I think I shall have it in here today."

She wanted to protest. She wanted to grab her dress. She wanted to tell him that she could not possibly enter the kitchen and face the chef as she was now, naked, but one look at Mr. Darby told her that was exactly what he expected.

She tried to cover herself with her hands but it was impossible. The chef looked at her then looked away, no more interested in Lily's nakedness than she was in Lily's clothed body. This should have eased Lily's tension and nerves, but it did nothing of the sort.

Instead, it made her fear grow. For if the chef was so unimpressed by the sight of a naked woman in the kitchen, shivering with fear, what other horrors might she be accustomed to?

Lily suddenly worried about the fate of all the girls who had doubtless come before her.

Chef filled the tray with Mr. Darby's lunch, a sandwich on thick slices of white bread, a tall glass of beer, a small bowl of olives and then, when Lily turned to leave, chef smacked her bottom with a wooden spoon, causing Lily to jump and nearly drop the tray she clutched in her hands.

The wooden spoon against her abused flesh stung angrily.

Mr. Darby was seated once more on the settee, speaking softly into the phone. He nodded towards the table and Lily set down his lunch, wishing that he would release her, that he would allow her to dress, but when she looked around for her dress, she realized it was gone. And with it, any foolish hope she may have harbored.

"Yes, I think you're quite right," he said into the phone, and she held her hands before her, clasped in front of her pubis in a useless attempt to mask her nakedness. "It's too early to know. She isn't ready."

She realized then that he was talking about her, that he

was not alone in this terrible secret.

That someone else knew about her shame.

She stared at the sandwich on the plate, willing herself not to cry.

"I'll let you know once I've made my decision."

Finally, he hung up the phone and addressed her. "You will sit in the armchair with your legs spread wide while I eat."

He motioned to a Louis XV chair with gold and green brocade upholstery. She did as he commanded, feeling the cool air of the room on her moist, exposed sex. When she put her hands to her lap, he snapped his fingers.

"Hands on the armrests. I want to see you."

So it began. The newest chapter of her time at Chateau Oriol. Lily did all that she could to satisfy his whims, but no matter what she did, no matter how she strived to please him, he found an excuse to punish her. She was a minute late with his coffee. She wasn't standing straight enough. Her apron was askew. It didn't matter. There was always something. His punishments varied. Some days, he used his hand. Others, he picked up the whip. Always, he delivered the blows to her naked flesh.

At times, he ordered her to the Game Room and there he had her strip naked. Sometimes, he would make her stand, naked, in the middle of the room while he pondered over the punishment she would receive, often musing aloud. Other times, he would have her lean over the desk in his office, and she'd stare out at the forested mountains that encircled them, wishing for freedom, as he struck her repeatedly.

He forced her to count each blow and thank he when her punishment was complete.

He never touched her expect to punish her. But he punished her regularly. And she learned to expect these punishments, just as before she learned to expect his critiques.

She sobbed. She wept. She cried out in pain but he showed no mercy, as if such sounds filled him with base satisfaction. She trembled with shame, with fear, with pain and also, to her great mortification, with need. A need so bleak and terrible, she could not admit even to herself.

At night, if she did not collapse immediately with exhaustion, she pleasured herself. She found her sex always wet and wanting, which only added to her shame.

Masturbation dulled the throb between her legs, but it brought her little pleasure.

9

The bell, ringing, summoned her. She took a deep breath, mentally going over what she could have possibly done wrong, but she could think of nothing.

Resigned, head hanging, she walked the long passageway to his study where she found him, standing before his desk, a glass of whiskey in one hand, a cigarette burning in the other.

"You may sit," he said dismissively, motioning towards the chair set in the middle of the room.

She sat with posture perfect and crossed her legs, staring at her hands on her lap.

"Look at me."

She lifted her gaze obediently. He stared at her intently and she shivered in response.

"Uncross your legs."

Knowing what would come if she disobeyed, she hastily uncrossed her legs. He smiled without warmth or kindness.

Something was coming. And she feared it. Just as she

craved the knowledge. And so she sat, waiting for him to decide while he sipped his whiskey and smoked his cigarette, occasionally flicking ash towards the ashtray.

"You surprise me," he said at last, his voice low and dangerous. It wasn't a question and so, she just stared at him, waiting. He seemed pleased by this, because he smiled again and offered her a drink.

"Sir?"

"A drink," he repeated patiently, as if addressing a child and not a grown woman.

Her mind scrambled. This had to be a trick. But she didn't know what he wanted and so, helplessly, she merely answered, "Okay."

He moved languidly to the bar and selected a crystal decanter she knew contained Scotch. She'd never tasted Scotch before and when he handed her the glass, she took it in her trembling hands.

"Drink."

And so she drank. The harsh liquor burned her throat, causing her to cough and sputter. She wiped the whiskey from her lips with the back of her hand and waited for his biting remarks.

"Finish it."

She pleaded with her eyes for mercy but there was no mercy in his expression.

Closing her eyes, she forced herself to drain the glass in a single swallow.

It stung her nostrils. Her throat felt raw.

He reached out his hand and obediently, she handed him the empty glass. Without taking his eyes off her, he placed it on the desk behind him.

"Did you enjoy that?"

She shook her head. "No, sir."

"Why did you drink it?"

"You told me to," she answered, ashamed by the truth of her response.

"Correct." He sipped his drink, momentarily lost in thought. "You finally seem to understand. You are to obey me, unquestioningly, in anything I ask."

She shook her head with mounting panic. "I don't understand anything, sir."

"You understand better than you realize."

She blinked in surprise. For a moment, she hesitated. But she had been silent too long. Curiosity burned her. "May I ask you something?"

He lifted one eyebrow in surprise, but then he nodded. Lily realized he was in a strange and unpredictable mood.

"Why am I really here?"

His slow smile filled Lily with dread. "To please me, of course." He put his glass down and stubbed out his cigarette and then crossed his arms over his chest, staring down at her. "Undress."

"But I've done nothing wrong," she protested, anticipating the punishment to come.

"Don't give me an excuse. I'm in a very cruel mood."

Lily came quickly to her feet, her whole body trembling like a brittle leaf in the wind.

Her fingers shook so much, she had a difficult time lowering the zipper on her dress. She forced her mind to go quiet as she removed her dress and folded it carefully and when he held out his hand, she passed it to him.

Standing before him in nothing but her corset, she fought the urge to cross her arms over her chest, knowing that was exactly what he wanted and expected from her.

An excuse. To punish her. To torment her. So she stood tall, her arms at her sides, her body on display.

"You have Charles to thank. I almost threw you out when he told me you were a virgin. But he has a good eye and suggested I keep you. I wonder if he was right." He circled her. "Remove your panties and give them to me."

He held out his hand and when he took her panties, he lifted them to his face, inhaling deeply.

"Just as I suspected," he murmured, his dark brown eyes meeting hers. And then he said the words she had been dreading since this whole ordeal began. "You like this."

She shook her head frantically.

"You're aroused. Look at this." He thrust her panties in her face and in shame, she saw the wetness there. "You're turned on."

She shook her head. "No."

"You're sopping wet. Admit it."

She refused to acknowledge what was so obvious to them both.

"Why are you doing this to me?" she sobbed.

"Because you were destined for this," he responded in a voice devoid of feeling. "Because you are like me, though you may never admit it. You fight it but your body betrays you. I can smell your cunt from across the room."

He reached out and with tenderness that made her recoil, he stroked her cheek like she was a delicate treasure. Without thinking, she leaned into his gentle caress. And just as quickly, he dropped his hand away and she felt the bitter loss of his touch.

"I'm tired of silly parlor games. Pretending that you don't want what I can give you." He stared at her, his chest pumping. She saw the excitement, the hunger. "On your knees."

The stern look he gave her made her obey. With the corset constricting her ribs, she was forced to bend her knees until they softly thudded against the ground. She steadied herself with her palms.

"Brigitte mentioned she saw you that night. That you watched. You dirty little spy. And then, you went upstairs and masturbated," he said, as if reading her thoughts.

He leaned against the desk, waiting. When Lily didn't move, his frustration only grew.

"Take out my cock!" he barked, his voice cold and hard.

"No."

The word echoed in the room. She glared at him. For a moment, Darby said nothing. And then his easy laughter washed over Lily.

"My little flower, no isn't a word I permit here."

When she didn't move, he grabbed her head roughly, his hands digging into her hair as he forced her forward. Without releasing her, he freed himself from the confines of his pants. She breathed him in. The dark and dangerous scent that reminded her of damp earth. His cock, mere inches from her face, was hard and thick. She'd never before seen one so close. She wetted her lips in fear.

He let out a low moan from the back of his throat when she opened her mouth tentatively, taking his head between her wet lips. And then he gripped her long blond hair, wrapping it around his thick wrist, forcing his cock deeper.

She struggled against him, but he was too strong as he held her tight, forcing her to accept him. He gave her no time to acclimate to his girth. Weeks of impatience were unleashed as he fucked her face roughly, pausing only to let her suck in a deep breath before he plunged deeper once more.

She could do nothing but accept the reality of her situation and pray that it would not last long. His moans of pleasure filled her ears, making her skin burn. Eventually, he slowed his thrusts, content to feel her warm mouth envelope him. He tightened his grip on her hair. She prayed he would find release soon and free her from her agony.

Tears streamed down her face. She sucked his cock as if her life depended on it.

With a groan, he pushed her away and she fell backwards, landing hard on her bruised ass, panting as tears stained her cheeks. His cock glistened with her saliva.

"I'll give you a choice," he whispered, pulling her roughly to her feet. "Would you like to keep your precious virginity a day longer?"

"Please," she sobbed. "I'm waiting…until marriage."

He laughed. "Well, that's certainly not going to happen. But I will give you another day if you'd like."

Chuckling, he wrapped his muscular arms around her, imprisoning her in his embrace. She buried her face in his chest, thankful not to be forced to look at him.

"I can take you here," he said, pressing his finger roughly against her asshole. She quivered, her whole body tensed with fear. She'd known, deep down, that this day would come.

That he wouldn't be content to simply beat her.

That he would want more.

That he would want everything.

But in her innocence, it never occurred to her that he might want her there as well.

"Will it hurt?" Her long eyelashes fluttered against her tear stained cheeks, like the dampened wings of a butterfly.

"Yes."

She shuddered in his arms. "Worse than the other way?"

He pressed harder, forcing her open, giving her a taste of the pain he promised. "Undoubtedly," he whispered in her ear, his hot breath sending a tingle down her spine. "The choice is yours. I will have you. Today. You must decide which hole I use. I won't often give you this option."

She tried to calm her thoughts, but fear clouded her judgment. How had she ever pitied this man? This monster?

"Decide or I'll take both your cunt and your ass."

"Please…" She sobbed into his chest.

Laughter rumbled through him. "Beg as much as you want, it won't make the slightest difference. I've waited long enough for this moment. I won't wait longer."

He continued probing her ass with his thick finger and she thought about his thick, heavy cock as it roughly took her throat.

"Take me the normal way," she said hoarsely as she swallowed her fear.

"You'll need to be more specific, as I assure you, both ways are completely normal."

"My vagina." She cringed at the word.

"Cunt."

"What?"

"You will call it your cunt. Understood?"

"Yes."

"Yes what?"

"Yes…*Sir*."

"Now, tell me again what you'd like me to do." He ran his hand lovingly over her hair.

A tear crept down her cheek. "Take my cunt." She buried her head in his chest in defeat.

"Such an innocent little flower," he whispered in her ear, his breath hot. She could feel his erection pressing into her stomach but with his arms around her, she could not escape.

She let out a sigh of relief when he withdrew his finger from her anus. He cupped her backside in his large, powerful hands, spreading her cheeks and Lily could feel the cool air of the room on her most private of parts.

He released her only to roughly penetrate her with two fingers, opening up her virgin sex. She bit her lip to stop from crying.

"Does that hurt?" he whispered in her ear. She heard the delighted arousal in his question and when he slapped her ass, hard, forcing his fingers deeper inside of her, she jumped.

"Does that hurt?" he whispered again.

She sobbed.

"Does it hurt?" he repeated forcefully.

"Yes," she sobbed into his chest.

Satisfied, he withdrew his fingers and then, without warning, he lifted her easily and deposited her hard on his desk, forcing the air from her lungs. She stared at him, panting, afraid.

He moved closer, his powerful body looming over her as he lifted her legs and wrapped them around his waist.

His cock nudged her wet opening.

For despite everything, she was hopelessly wet.

With his eyes locked on hers, he impaled her with a single thrust, and Lily screamed in pain as she felt herself being torn apart.

He did not move. Pain filled her.

"Keep your legs around my waist," he bit out roughly.

She sobbed but kept her legs tight around his waist, afraid of what might happen if she disobeyed.

He reached into her corset, pulling her breasts up and free. He stroked her nipples to hard points.

And then, satisfied, he reached between them and found her clit, rubbing it softly.

The sensation was unlike anything she'd felt before. Heightened. Sharp. Painful. Yet also, pleasurable.

"You will come," he said roughly and she cried harder.

He couldn't do this. And yet, she felt her cunt get wet, the feeling of his fingers on her clit causing her body to soften around him.

"Yes, that's better," he encouraged her. "Come for me, my little flower. Show me how much you want this. How much you need this."

With his other hand, he stroked her cheek, wiping away her tears.

She cried as her body betrayed her. The walls of her sex went slick around the hard cock buried inside her. His expert fingers gave her no reprieve as he coaxed her closer to the edge.

She came, sobbing, her orgasm ripped from her body as her cunt spasmed around him. Only when she stopped shaking did he begin to fuck her in earnest. He fucked her hard, with savage purpose, and she submitted, helpless to fight him off, sobbing the whole time.

And when he came, filling her cunt with his seed, she wept louder. His cock was still hard when he withdrew and pushed her to her knees.

"Clean me off."

Cum dripped from her pussy as she took him into her mouth, tasting their combined juices and the hint of blood, like a copper penny, knowing he had cruelly ripped through her maidenhead. She gagged but the protest inside of her had dried up, leaving only a strange sense of calm. Like she was floating far away from this scene.

Eventually, he pulled her to her feet and she stumbled again. With surprising tenderness, he brushed the tears from her face and gazed into her eyes with an expression she could only describe as compassionate.

"You are mine," he whispered fiercely. "Your pleasure. Your pain. Your very existence."

She did not fight him. In this moment, she knew what he said was true.

"That means your orgasms are mine as well. I know everything that happens here. I know you go to your room and finger fuck yourself like a greedy little slut. That ends today. You will not be allowed to pleasure yourself unless I say so." He stroked her face lovingly and she closed her eyes, letting him soothe her with his gentle touch. "I had this designed especially for you."

Lily opened her eyes. Behind him, on the desk, she saw something that made her shiver.

"A chastity belt," he explained. "You will wear it until I decide you're obedient enough to go without." He held it up for Lily to see and her eyes widened and her mouth parted, but she did not speak. There, nestled in the leather harness that would cover her sex, she saw two small dildos. "It is designed to hold a dildo in both your cunt and your anus. Now turn around."

She began to cry again in earnest as he bent her over his desk. She felt something cold and slippery between her ass cheeks and then his long fingers pushing inside of her, the pain exquisitely sharp as he stretched her.

She sighed with relief when he withdrew only to yelp in surprise when he forced something hard and long into her abused passage.

He then helped her into the chastity belt. The small dildo slipped easily into her recently sexed cunt. Though it was not much longer than his index finger, its presence was unforgettable.

The stiff leather belt fit snug around her hips.

Lily's heart sank at the sound of the tiny padlock being locked into place. The sound was like a prison door closing.

Mr. Darby leaned back, admiring his work as his fingers absentmindedly caressed her hip. The smile he gave her was pure satisfaction.

"There are two keys. I have one," he said, holding out his hand, letting Lily see the small key that rested in his palm. "Tomas has the other. If you need to use the restroom, you will ask one of us to remove the chastity belt."

She sobbed.

"There, there. It isn't too bad," he cooed, patting her cheek.

Her mind raced, struggling to digest the change in her circumstances. She tossed and turned in her bed, but sleep would not deliver her from her tormented thoughts. Even after the explosive climax earlier, she felt undone. Tightly strung. Burnt out. Her anus was stretched around the unrelenting toy. Her sex clenched around the miniature cock that filled her cunt without satisfaction or pleasure.

The frustration she felt, the need, consumed her. She thought only of sex. Of release. Every time she rolled over, the dildos shifted inside of her, causing her to weep with frustration.

Finally, just as the sun was about to rise in the sky, sleep came. A blessing. But it brought no relief. She dreamed of being fucked.

When she awoke, the sheets clung to her sweat slicked skin and her bladder pushed uncomfortably against the stiff leather chastity belt. Her face burned with humiliation, knowing what she had to do, but she couldn't hold off any longer.

With heavy steps, she went in search of Mr. Darby, knowing she would never be able to ask Tomas to free her. She prayed Darby would see her suffering and take pity on her and free her from this cruel device.

But deep down she understood her torment was only now beginning.

She was not wrong.

10

For one week, Lily suffered terribly. In the morning, after Mr. Darby released her and stood, waiting, outside the bathroom while she washed up, he would then take her over his knee and replace the dildos. Every day, the size of the phallus in her ass increased and with it, her torment.

All the while, her body, so tightly wrung, ached for something Lily had no word for. Her nipples were sharp points, visible through her dress. She continued to wear her corset, holding her posture perfectly erect. She moved with difficulty, a fact Mr. Darby pointed out to her regularly.

Wielding a riding crop, he forced her to walk across his office again and again.

"You're not a bloody milk maid clomping around in the muck!" he'd shout, landing the riding crop hard on her ass and causing her uneven gait to falter. "You look ghastly. You are to seduce me with your body. Your hips must sway pleasantly. Again!"

She struggled to please him. To walk with a natural

grace made impossible by the stiff corset and dildos that filled her but brought her no pleasure.

The leather chastity belt absorbed much of the sting, and it was not nearly as bad as when he hit her bare bottom. But each blow made her trip and forced her ass to clench around the dildo that speared it.

"Provoke me! Arouse me! It's like watching a cow chomp its way across a field. Again!"

Again and again, he tormented her until he was red in the face and Lily felt as if she could not take another step.

For with every step, her arousal grew. The leather pressed against her clitoris in such a way that it left her panting, but without release. It did not matter how she tried to move, how she tried to contort herself to find that perfect spot. It did not exist.

She wept with frustration and need.

For a week, he fucked only her mouth. When he finished parading her around the house, raining blows of the crop down on her ass, he made her get down on her hands and knees and take his cock in her mouth.

Sometimes, he came deep in her throat and she barely tasted his cum. Other times, he'd withdraw and instruct her to stick out her tongue and he would take himself in his hands, fisting his erection, until he exploded on her tongue.

He came on her tits. On her back. On her buttocks. Not an inch of her body was spared this humiliation. Of being marked by him. For it was obvious, even to Lily, that he was marking her. Like a wild animal might relieve himself at the foot of a tree.

And though her frustration increased by the hour, Lily refused to beg this cruel man to take pity on her and let her come. Though she thought about it constantly. For how could she not?

On the eighth day, Lily awoke to find Darby standing at the foot of her bed. Beneath the placid expression he wore, she could see almost a hint of satisfaction. Or pride.

She did not bother to pull her sheets up to cover her nakedness. He had seen everything before. And it would do nothing to protect her.

She expected him to order her out of bed. Instead, he came to sit beside her, trapping her between his muscular body and the wall.

He stroked her hair. He brushed her cheeks with his thumbs. For hands that usually delivered such pain, they could be so gentle at times. Like he was tending to a wounded bird that had fallen from its nest, afraid that he might break her fragile, hollow bones.

She blinked up at him expectantly. Waiting for whatever was to come. Whatever invisible transgression that would cause him to punish her next.

Instead, he smiled. A slow radiant smile that extended to his rich brown eyes.

For the first time, she noticed the flecks of gold.

He had truly beautiful eyes.

Rarely was she given an opportunity to examine him so closely or for so long. She took it. Breathed it in. Reveled in his handsome appearance and this unexpected moment of kind reprieve.

Morning filtered through the curtain, illuminating her little attic room. But there was no urgency. No rush. They sat in silence, watching each other, considering each other.

This was different from how they normally were. Him, sitting beside her, almost as if they were equals.

Finally, he opened his hand. There, resting in his palm, was the little key that could free her from her prison.

"Should I unlock you?"

Her pale pink lips parted, but there did not exist the words to describe how much she wanted her freedom. Freedom from this dreaded contraption that kept her in a constant state of arousal. Constantly desiring a release she would never be allowed. Not without his express permission. Permission that Lily knew would never be granted.

This desire was far worse than the lashes he delivered. Worse than the humiliation of being forced to suck his cock and accept his cum wherever he saw fit. For they both knew the truth. That every time she took him in her mouth, her cunt flooded with heat. That though he was her torturer, he was also the one man who could set her free.

"And why did I make you wear the chastity belt?" he asked in the voice of a stern but patient teacher.

She glanced wistfully at the key before looking up at him and answering, "To teach me that I must never come without your permission."

He cocked his head, his expression showing that he was pleased with the concise answer she had given. "Do you think you have learned your lesson?"

"Yes, sir."

"I would like to free you," he said thoughtfully, "but I am not sure you're ready."

Lily pushed aside her blankets and sat up, driving the dildos deeper. She sucked in a sharply, but ignored the sensation. The need.

"Please, sir. I'll do anything you ask, just please, free

me," she begged, placing her hands imploringly on his knees. "Please, let me go and I will do exactly as you ask. Anything you ask."

He cupped her cheek and she leaned into his palm. All she could think about was being free of the dreaded device that kept her tossing and turning most of the night, that kept her mind constantly on the juncture of her thighs and that ball of nerve endings that begged, pleaded, screamed for attention.

"If you fail to obey me, I will know."

She shook her head adamantly. "I won't disappoint you."

"The punishment would be both swift and painful."

She nodded in understanding. She wouldn't touch herself. Not as long as he freed her. Not as long as he took these dreaded dildos from her body.

He stood and pulled her to her feet. She stumbled, falling against his chest, inhaling the scent of him. Of cigarette smoke and expensive cologne. He slipped his arm under her, lifting her with ease and she rested her cheek against his chest and let her eyes close.

She didn't open her eyes until he eased her out of his arms and onto the porcelain vanity in the bathroom. She bit her lip as he inserted the lock and she let out a sigh of relief when she heard it click open.

He pulled her off the vanity and then removed the belt and the two dildos and the relief that Lily felt was only momentary. For she suddenly realized how empty she felt. An emptiness that was not only physical, but existed somewhere deep within her core. A spiritual emptiness that caused her a moment's panic.

He cupped her chin, forcing her to meet his eyes. And

what she saw there was something that approached respect. It didn't make sense, but that was what she thought she saw, gone again in an instant.

"You may perform your ablutions, but I will be waiting in the hall and the door shall remain open a crack."

She sagged with relief when she was finally alone. Glancing at the door, cracked open, she perched on the toilet, but though she needed to go, it took a long while, knowing that Darby could hear every sound she made.

And when she'd flushed the toilet and was washing her hands, he returned, coming up behind her and pulling her back against his chest.

For a moment, they stood like that. Her back pressed against his chest and she could feel the steady rhythm of his breathing, his heartbeat, could feel his fingers, surprisingly gentle where they rested on her hips. But just as she was beginning to relax into the familiarity of this position, he flipped her around.

He cupped her sex roughly and Lily couldn't help but moan. Her body craved release. And though cruel, though unbelievably cruel, Lily knew what pleasure his hands could bring her.

He smiled, unable to resist the urge to toy with the petite woman in front of him. When he slapped her sex lightly, she jumped, but did not utter a sound.

"Take a seat on the edge of the tub and spread your legs. We need to shave you. This," he waved dismissively at her thatch of blond pubic hair, "cannot continue."

He let the shower run, filling the room with thick, fragrant steam. And then he knelt before her and with the flick of his wrist, opened a straight razor.

Lily shook, seeing the glint of the blade, her eyes wide,

her mouth hanging open.

Seeing her terror, he placed one hand on her knee and squeezed gently. "I won't hurt you, my little flower, I promise."

She took a deep breath and urged herself to relax. But she kept her eyes closed, afraid that she might flinch when the blade drew close to her delicate skin, causing him to nick her unintentionally.

With expert attention, he shaved her completely bare, pulling at the lips of her cunt to examine them closer, to ensure that every hair was removed. And when he finished, he went to the vanity and from it removed a crystal bottle and he patted the scented oil onto her sex and she sucked in a hiss of air as it stung and burned.

He stood back, admiring his handiwork. "Very good. This is how you shall remain for the duration of your time here. If I feel so much as the slightest stubble or hair, I will string you up and punish you."

She nodded and he smiled, a rare dazzling smile that made her momentarily forget that she was, in fact, his prisoner, and he, her tormentor.

"Good. Shower and change and when you are finished, meet me in the Game Room for today's lesson."

11

Lily stood in the center of the Game Room as Mr. Darby went to the locked cupboard where he kept his toys. She couldn't believe how the simple act of shaving her sex bare could so completely change her perception, and yet, it did. The walk downstairs had caused her naked folds to rub together sensually.

She felt voluptuous. Carnal.

She felt alive.

Looking at Darby, his strong back to her, it was hard to believe that he had changed her so completely. She came to him an inexperienced virgin and now…she shivered, her body hot and yearning.

"Obey me and you will be rewarded. Disobey and you will be punished," he intoned in a quiet voice that radiated power. Her pulse raced as she went over the last few hours in her head. She'd done nothing to disobey him, nothing she could remember, and yet, if he wanted he could find the slightest infraction.

With a gentle hand, he brushed her hair behind her ear.

And then he stroked the pad of his thumb over the swell of her lower lip and without thinking, she opened her mouth.

When he pushed his thumb into her mouth, she sucked it hungrily, careful to only lightly graze her teeth over his skin the way she knew he liked.

"Today, you pleased me. Your demeanor upstairs, your eagerness to satisfy me, these are the attributes I look for in a girl. My methods can be, at times, harsh, but how else will you learn? It's time you learn the pleasure you can experience when you've pleased me."

With a wet popping sound, he pulled his thumb from her mouth and she nearly pouted at the loss.

"There are so many things for you to learn. So very many things indeed. But we shall start with a simple lesson." As he spoke, he walked around her and she heard him gently pull down the zipper on her dress. It fell around her ankles and she stepped out of it gracefully. "How did the chastity belt make you feel?"

She didn't think before answering. She was past thinking. Past considering what affect his actions were having on her and what that meant. "Frustrated," she admitted in a voice that did not tremble. "Also, aroused."

She could hear him smiling when he said, "And now, how do you feel?"

She scanned her body as she considered her response and realized, without surprise, that her answer remained the same. "Frustrated and aroused."

"Would you like me to do something about that?"

She had to angle her head back to meet Darby's eyes. She knew that after this moment there would be no going back. She knew, also, the pleasure he was capable of delivering.

For a split second, she hesitated. "Yes, please." And then, she added, "Sir."

The smile he gave her warmed her. A genuine smile. Not forced. Not condescending. He looked...delighted. As if her answer came as a pleasant surprise.

She shivered in anticipation.

He kept his eyes fixed on hers as he ran a single finger over her bare sex and she bit the inside of her cheek, her blue eyes opening wider. It felt...luxurious. The feel of his finger against her naked flesh, no hair standing in the way. It felt...silky smooth and elegant.

Her cunt was wet. Her skin burned as though with fever. A week of servicing him, a week of constant penetration without release, and now, his single digit, running along her seam so slowly.

It was torture. But of the most delicious variety.

The type of torture that made it all worthwhile.

"For someone with so little experience, you're delightfully responsive," he said, his tone thoughtful and without judgment. "I'd like to test how responsive."

For a brief moment, he cupped her cheek tenderly and she leaned into his hand, the touch so soft and gentle and unexpected. Through her fogged brain, it occurred to her how starved she was for human kindness. But just as soon, he withdrew his hand, leaving her aching for more.

When he spoke again, all kindness was gone from his voice causing Lily to wonder if she'd imagined it. "Eyes on the floor. Hands out."

She offered him her hands, palms lifted to the sky, like a prayer. Her eyelashes batted her cheeks as she struggled to remain calm. She made no sound when he clipped the cool leather cuffs around her slender wrists.

He connected the cuffs, locking her wrists together, then tugged her towards the settee.

"Arms above your head."

Lily balanced at the edge of the settee, arms raised as Darby crouched in front of her. He pushed her legs apart. She felt the leather cuff around her ankle and then he clipped it to the leg of the settee. He then repeated the process with her other ankle.

Her arms strained as she held them above her head.

And then he fastened them to something that dangled from the ceiling.

She found herself locked in place, unable to move, on full display.

Only now did she notice the items lain out on the table before her. The phalluses of different shapes, made from different materials. And other things, things she did not recognize.

She struggled against her bonds but could not break free. Panic filled her chest. He'd promised pleasure, promised release, but suddenly, she wasn't so certain. Suddenly, she worried if she had trusted too soon, too eagerly.

Mr. Darby crouched down, his sensual lips so close to her exposed sex and when he blew a thin stream of air on her sex, her body tensed.

In fear.

In arousal.

Without looking away from her sex, he told her she was free to make any sound she pleased, but to know it would make no difference in what he did to her.

He opened her first with his fingers, long thick fingers

that pushed and probed her and she felt her body betray her. Somewhere in the back of her mind, she knew this was wrong. But there could be no denying her body's response.

When he rubbed her clit, she moaned, unable to hold back. After he'd denied her all week, even the lightest touch felt electric. When she felt his tongue, hot and rough against her clit, she screamed.

He teased and tortured her and she pulled at her restraints, but it was hopeless. She was trapped. All she could do was let go and feel.

She whimpered when he ceased to touch her. With eyes barely able to focus, she watched him reach for a long metal dildo. He rubbed it along her sex, causing her to spasm, and when he slowly inserted it, the metal cooled her burning cunt but did nothing to temper the need building inside her.

He toyed with her.

He played with her.

Again and again he brought her to the edge of climax before leaning back and watching her, amusement glistening in his deep brown eyes.

She forgot the respectable virgin she once was. She begged. She pleaded. For him to release her. For him to finish her off. For him to fuck her. For him to rip her apart with his cock. For anything but this exquisite torture. This maddening anticipation.

Sweat glistened on her naked skin. Her muscles ached. But she cared only about her sex. Only about the pleasure being denied to her.

He abandoned the metal dildo and picked up a thick, glass dildo and eased it into her. She arched her back, urging it deeper. Lust obliterated shame. She mewled loudly.

When he finally held a vibrator to her clit as he fucked her with an enormous glass cock, she came violently, screaming as pleasure ripped through her. She expected him to stop then, but he didn't. He continued pressing the vibrator to her clit, continued fucking her.

She came again.

And again.

She came until her body felt like it was being torn violently apart.

She barely registered him releasing her and she sank into the settee, her body spent, her mind liquid.

But he wasn't finished. He lifted her easily. She felt his hard cock press against her and could not resist when he pushed into her dripping sex. He fucked her slowly, gently, then withdrew.

She whimpered.

And then he lifted her once more and bent her over the back of the settee and she felt his cock, wet with her arousal, press against her back passage, and she was too tired, too spent, to fight him off.

He took her violently. A week of stretching had not prepared her for the sharp pain as he pushed into her for the first time, robbing her of her last vestige of virginity. She didn't think she was capable of another orgasm, but when he began expertly manipulating her clit, she howled as pleasure once more overtook her. And when he filled her with his liquid, she felt only a strange tranquility blanketing her.

If Lily thought he was finished with her, she was sorely mistaken. He continued his sensual abuse for the duration of the day until Lily lapsed into unconsciousness.

Lily awoke, alone, in a room that was not hers, enveloped in soft, costly cotton sheets and fluffy down. She stretched her aching limbs, enjoying the sensual feeling of the sheets against her naked flesh.

For she was still naked.

She sat up and took in her surroundings. A room where she had never been before. One of the second floor bedrooms. The walls were painted a rich royal blue and she was tucked into an enormous four-post bed. The room exuded quiet extravagance.

Looking around, she expected to find Darby, but he was gone. She was alone.

On the bedside table, she noticed a single white bloom. A calla lily in a blue glass vase. She pressed her nose to the bloom and inhaled.

For a moment, she considered returning to her room. But she quickly dismissed the thought and sank deeper into the bed, stretching her limbs wide and smiling.

Images flashed in her mind. Darby, naked, his powerful physique as he ravaged her. Again and again until she drifted off to sleep.

He'd brushed her hair from her face. He'd whispered in her ear. She felt, for the first time, truly safe.

The ringing of the bell. The morning routine. She brought Darby his coffee and his newspaper, feeling like a nervous schoolgirl after the day and night they'd shared. He'd awoken in her something that scared her. But also, excited her. Her hands trembled as she looked at him in expectation.

Waiting for him to speak.

Waiting for him to address her.

To address what had passed between them. The passion he had unleashed.

Instead, he unfolded the newspaper and leaned back in his chair.

Lily's entrails twisted in humiliation.

Had she imagined it?

Had it been a cruel and magical dream brought about by all her prolonged suffering?

But no. She'd awoken in that beautiful blue bedroom instead of her grim little room on the third floor. And her body, it showed all the signs of wear. The aches that she could feel deep inside of her. All the places he had touched that no one had touched before.

It wasn't a dream. Of that she was certain.

She wanted to speak up. Wanted to pressure him into acknowledging her. But she remembered his warning. Obey him and be rewarded. Disobey and be punished.

She feared his lashes as much as she craved his acceptance.

She stared at her feet in silence and waited.

As he ignored her.

Finally, when Lily felt as if she might begin to cry, he said, "You may go."

She held her head high as she left the room.

She refused to show him how much his indifference cut at her.

12

Lily scrubbed the kitchen floor angrily. Her muscles protested every pass of the coarse brush, but she pushed on, needing this to try to banish the thoughts from her mind.

How could she want him after everything he'd done? How could she ache for him? After weeks of abuse, after a day of sensual torture, this silence was the worst punishment he could have dealt her.

Every time she thought about it, tears burned her eyes and so she scrubbed the floor harder, until her palms felt raw.

She scrubbed as if her life depended on it. She didn't care that anyone walking past could see up her skirt at her naked and abused bottom. She didn't care that everyone in this dreaded house knew her torture.

She didn't care that Tomas was likely laughing at her at this very moment. That man hated her from the moment she arrived and he probably thought she deserved everything she got at the hands of Mr. Darby.

How could she explain she wanted whatever he would give her, anything but this indifference?

She tossed the coarse brush in the bucket, sloshing dirtied water onto the newly cleaned tile floor.

She cursed under her breath. She was almost too tired to care.

"I don't pay you to be sloppy."

Lily's heart swelled at the sound of Darby's stern voice. She looked up through the hair that spilled in front of her face to find him standing in front of her, his hands on his hips as he looked down at her.

She had to suppress the smile that threatened to break across her face.

Instead, she looked back down at the floor, mumbling her apology. She didn't want him to know how much his sudden appearance affected her. How even his cruel words filled her now with joy.

He dropped a rag on the floor. "Clean that up immediately."

Eagerly, she did as he demanded, feeling his gaze upon her as she scrambled forward, her knees bruised from the hard tiled floor.

When the floor was dry, she looked up at him expectantly to find him frowning, his eyes narrowed.

"In my office. Now!"

Lily stood before him, hands in front of her, chastised as he paced in front of the window, smoking a cigarette.

Finally, he stopped pacing and turned to face her.

"Eyes up!"

She stared him in the eyes nervously, watching his face soften slightly.

"How are you feeling?" he asked gruffly. For a moment, Lily's heart stilled.

"I'm fine, sir."

The hard slap he delivered to her cheek made her eyes smart and she stumbled back.

"Never lie to me!"

She trembled in fear. "I'm sorry, sir."

"I have no interest in your insipid apologies. Tell me the truth. How are you feeling?"

She rubbed her cheek. "Sore. My whole body hurts." He'd never slapped her before.

"Better," he responded, leaning against his desk. "What else?"

"Hurt," she answered, unable to hide the truth from him.

"How so?"

"Today, when you refused to even look at me, I thought I'd imagined everything. I thought—" Here she hesitated before continuing, her face burning hot, "I thought you no longer wanted me."

"That upset you?" A strange note crept into his voice. As if her answer surprised him.

Finally, he shook his head, dismissing it. But the look remained. As if, somehow, she baffled him.

It was a look she'd never expected to see on his face.

"May I ask you a question?" she asked hesitantly. He watched her through narrowed eyes before finally nodding. "What do you want from me?"

His eyes flicked across her skin and when he licked his lower lip before speaking, Lily felt as though he were licking her. "Everything."

That one word was all she needed. One word that

confirmed that the night before hadn't been a dream, some make believe, but real. So real. Her body ached from it, but that wasn't enough. Feeling suddenly brazen from his answer, Lily took a step forward and looked up at him with her eyes wide. "And what do you want from me now, sir?"

He studied her and she could only hope that she hadn't made a fatal miscalculation. But desperation clouded her judgment. She needed to feel his skin against hers, even if it was in punishment. She needed his reassurance even if that meant the crop.

"You fought me and yet, here you are, offering yourself to me like a sacrificial lamb," he said at last, his mouth quirked with amusement. "Delightfully compliant," he added. "If I told you to get undressed, would you?"

"Of course."

"And if I told you to spread yourself for me over this desk, would you?"

Again, she nodded.

"And if I told you to go to the Game Room and fetch me a cane, so I may beat you, would you do that as well?"

She trembled, but again, nodded. For though the cane filled her with fear, the idea of Mr. Darby touching her, in any way that he saw fit, still made her body come to life.

He leaned thoughtfully against the desk as he considered her responses and his many options. For she had realized, in that moment, that his options were limitless. Because she would have complied with any of them, no matter what. No matter how damning.

She recognized then that she both loved and hated the power he wielded over her so easily, and so she stood before him and waited for him to decide how next to torment her.

For even the pleasure he dealt was torturous. And that made it all the more powerful.

"Undress and crawl to the Game Room on your hands and knees. In the locked cupboard you will find a large dildo and a glass butt plug. Fetch them."

She was undressing before he'd finished speaking and when she was on her hands and knees on the carpeted floor, he crouched beside her, placing his large hand on the flat of her back, stilling her.

"You will need the key."

She felt him reach between her legs and insert a cold, hard metal object into her cunt. From it dangled the heavy chain that dragged on the floor and when he slapped her ass, firmly but not to cause pain, she began to crawl, and she could hear the chain dragging behind her on the floor.

She crawled with a singular purpose, crawled, keeping her eyes on the floor, hoping she would not run into Tomas. But she was not so lucky, and when she crawled through the large entryway on her way to the Game Room, she caught sight of his shoes. He stood near the stairs, watching her slow progress.

"*Puta*," he snickered, not bothering to hide his contempt. Whore. She paid him no attention, for this was what Mr. Darby wanted and it was Mr. Darby whom she served, and not Tomas.

Still, her cheeks burned.

In the Game Room, the worn carpet felt pleasing upon her bruised knees. She found the cupboard easily, for she had seen Darby removing many things from it before. Blushing, she reached between her legs and yanked on the chain, extracting the key from her cunt. The heavy skeleton key glistened with her arousal. But she was too focused to feel embarrassment. Instead, she sucked it clean, afraid the lock might stick otherwise.

She did not stand. She came up on her knees and inserted the key into the lock, hearing it click open as she turned it, and then she stared inside at the various sex toys that lay in wait.

She wished to try them all. Wished that he would try them all on her so she knew what to fear and what to yearn for, but it was not her place to ask for such things. So she found what he'd requested and closed the door, locking up its treasures once again.

It was not until she turned that she realized her predicament. He'd instructed her to crawl. But crawling, she had no use of her hands and so, how would she carry the toys?

She stared at them as she considered her options. She could, of course, put the butt plug into her bottom, but she cringed at the thought. It was one thing for Mr. Darby to violate her most inviolate of holes and quite another for her to do it of her own volition.

Dismissing the idea, she slid the butt plug easily into her cunt, tightening her muscles to hold it in place. The dildo she held between her teeth. It stretched her jaw painfully wide, but there was no other way. The chain on which the key rested she slipped around her neck. And thus, cunt filled, mouth stretched, key dragging noisily on the floor, she crawled back to Mr. Darby.

He said nothing but she sensed his approval in his silence.

She stopped and waited for him to do something, say something, breathing heavily around the dildo between her teeth. She could feel spit collecting at the corners of her mouth and she wanted nothing more than to brush it away, but she did not.

She heard his heavy foot falls and then felt him crouched behind her. He reached roughly between her legs and yanked the glass object from her cunt and she cringed at the lewd popping sound that it produced.

"For someone so inept, you are a fast learner," he said.

Lily heard only his praise.

Roughly, he lubricated her anus with her wetness and she bit harder on the toy between her teeth to stop herself from making a sound. He was no more gentle when he shoved the glass butt plug into her, stretching and filling her poor roughly-used asshole. But she did not complain.

"A woman of your nature looks best when properly abused," he said thoughtfully. "Don't you agree?"

Unable to speak with the dildo in her mouth, she could only nod her head in agreement, making him chuckle. He removed the dildo from her aching jaw and shoved it roughly into her cunt and she could not bite back the scream that escaped her lips.

"You will want to clench down because the punishment for letting that slip out will be severe."

With that, he patted her behind, a loving pat, and she clenched down in reflex, filled to the breaking point.

He stood in front of her and unzipped his fly and she knew what was expected. She gazed up at him before taking him into her mouth. Now every one of her holes was filled.

She sucked him as she knew he expected. And when she heard him call out Tomas' name, color stained her cheeks, but she could not protest with his cock lodged in her throat.

She heard the door open and close and Tomas' footsteps.

"Before I bought Chateau Oriol, the previous owner kept horses. I have it on good authority that Tomas can handle a riding crop like a master."

She squeezed her eyes shut, squeezed every muscle in her body, feeling the large dildo slip a millimeter out.

"Would you like a demonstration of his skill?"

A tear trickled out of the corner of her eye but she never stopped sucking his cock. She knew that Tomas could see her, could see the toys lodged inside of her, and that he would punish her severely because he hated her. Hated her for no reason, for not fault of her own.

There would be no kindness in the blows he delivered. There would be no pleasure at the end of the pain. There would only be his cruelty. His meanness. His hatred.

Lily accepted this. Accepted her humiliation at the hands of Mr. Darby, hoping that it would be worth it.

The first strike of the riding crop jolted her forward and she had to be careful that she did not bite Mr. Darby by mistake.

It took several cracks of the crop for Lily to find her rhythm and so it went, her sucking Mr. Darby's impressive erection as Tomas rained blows down on her tender, exposed flesh.

Mr. Darby was right. Tomas knew how to wield the crop with force and precision.

She closed her eyes, focusing all her attention on Mr. Darby's pleasure. On his moans. She tried not to think of the pain, and soon, she found she was able to block it out, centering her thoughts on the throbbing between her legs.

He came with a grunt, deep in her throat, and she swallowed everything, hungrily, greedily.

He pulled his cock from her lips with a wet sucking sound that made her humiliation complete.

Only moments later did she realize that Tomas had stopped striking her.

Darby patted her head like she was a faithful dog then walked towards the door. She heard Tomas panting from the exertion required to wield the crop for so long and so hard and then, her whole body turned to ice when Mr. Darby said, casually, as if he were merely commenting on the weather or the color of her dress, "You will take care of Tomas now."

She heard him yank down his zipper and then he shoved his cock rudely in her face. Her lips parted in surprise and Tomas took that opportunity to plunder her mouth. She gagged on the taste of perspiration that clung to him as he fucked her mouth eagerly and without remorse.

She wept, unable and unwilling to mask her misery. She would not let this horrible man think she enjoyed this.

At least he did not make her swallow his seed. Instead, with a grunt that made her skin crawl, he pulled out and she felt the hot streams of cum splash across her face, her cheeks and drip to the floor.

He laughed.

"Clean that up," he said before walking out and slamming the door.

Lily wept, curled up in her bed, facing the wall. She wept at Darby's cruelty. In the meanness that allowed him, no, compelled him, to lend her to Tomas. Tomas, who he must know hated her. She'd come to him that morning eager to serve him. Eager for his tutelage.

Now, she wanted nothing more than to strip the memories of the past twelve hours and everything that came before from her mind.

Her throat burned. The humiliation she felt went deep, staining everything. She wished she could forget, but she would never be able to forget the way Tomas looked down at her. Like she was dirt.

She was almost surprised when he didn't spit on her face.

She'd run to the bathroom and retched over the toilet, but nothing but bile came up. It didn't matter how long she let the shower run, the feeling remained. She felt sticky, dirty, used.

She froze when her bedroom door creaked opened. She knew without turning that it was Darby and she refused to give him the satisfaction of seeing her move towards him.

She continued staring at the blank wall. After several minutes of tense silence, filled only with her hoarse crying, the door shut. She sighed with relief. And then Darby's weight shifted the mattress as he came to sit beside her. She pulled away instinctively, trying to make herself smaller.

"Hush, little flower." He stroked her back with fingers so impossibly gentle, causing her to cry harder. He leaned down and she flinched, pulling away, refusing to look at him.

"Hush, now. You're okay," he cooed.

Lily hated him in this moment more than she'd ever hated him before. Hated the way she yearned to turn to him, yearned to let him heal her wounds. Wounds he inflicted.

No. She refused. She would not.

She did not move when he eased the sheets from her shoulders and traced her spine with his hands, large, flat palms that warmed her.

She felt a stirring in her loins and squeezed her eyes shut, refusing to believe her body could react to this man after everything he'd subjected her to.

"Little flower," he whispered, his breath hot and damp on her neck, causing her nipples to harden. "Don't fight me. Don't shut me out. Please."

For a moment, confused, disoriented, she felt as though she was the one who had wronged. She knew this was all some horrible game he was playing. That he would force her to welcome him into her arms, only to be pushed aside, reminded of her place.

She was his whore. His maid. The *puta* servant girl with nowhere to run.

Lily sobbed as he continued to gently stroke her skin. His strong fingers closed around her shoulders and he gently coaxed her onto her back, forcing her to look at him.

In the dim light of her bedroom, he looked like a fairytale prince. His strong jaw. His dark eyes surprisingly kind. His hair mussed.

She longed to run her fingers through his hair, to know if it was truly as soft as it appeared.

He gave her a slow smile that seemed to encourage such thoughts. Lily yanked her hand back when she realized she had been reaching for him.

When he leaned down, she almost expected to feel his

lips on hers and she realized that not once, in all their savage couplings, in all his torment, had he ever pressed his lips to hers and kissed her.

He'd bitten her shoulder.

Had licked her sex.

But he'd never once kissed her mouth.

The kiss never came.

"Hush, now," he whispered in her ear as he snaked his hand down her body, caressing her as he went, cupping her breasts, his thumb brushing her nipples to sharp, hard points, before he continued his slow exploration.

Before this moment, she knew sex only to be frantic, savage, brutal and so, Lily had no manner to process what she was experiencing, his light touch and gentle caresses, the way he smoothed her skin and whispered in her ear.

When he found her sex, it was already wet and hot. Lily's sobs turned to soft moans.

He stroked her carefully, bringing her much pleasure.

She moaned when he stood abruptly and she watched in wonder as he striped naked, revealing in the dusky light his magnificent form. His muscular chest with its fine covering of dark hair, his broad shoulders, his powerful thighs.

And between them, his cock, hard and proud against his flat stomach.

She would never get used to the magnificent sight of his body.

He crawled over her, pressing his hands into the mattress on either side of her head, trapping her. With one knee, he nudged her legs apart and she did not fight him. She watched him in awe, her mouth parted as if about to say something but suddenly, caught in the moment, no longer able to recall the words she'd once thought so necessary.

His sex brushed against hers, teasing, hot, hard.

Lily didn't mean to arch her hips off the mattress, but she did, her body following its own commands.

He entered her only an inch and waited, the muscles of his arms tense as he held himself poised above her.

She stared into his eyes as if staring into the eyes of a stranger.

He lowered himself slowly, his cock filling her exquisitely, and kissed her face, her neck, her jaw as he buried himself in her.

Her arms came around him, holding him tight to her body. She never wanted to let go. Never wanted to forget this feeling.

She decided, in this moment, that she would enjoy whatever pleasure he could give her and pretend that he was some stranger, some distant lover, someone who might even care for her.

The sex was slow and powerful. Darby let Lily come first, and it was her body undulating beneath him that brought his own climax.

For a breathless moment, they lay together, a tangle of sweaty limbs, in her narrow bed, both panting, his cock still hard inside of her.

The moment felt exquisitely tender to Lily, who knew nothing of true tenderness.

And when he pulled out and quickly dressed, she stared after him, too confused to speak.

What would she have said? Would she have begged for him to remain with her?

13

If Lily's time at Chateau Oriol taught her anything, it was to expect nothing, for Darby's behavior was constantly changing. The ground beneath her feet may as well have been wet sand or muddy earth. There were no sure-footed steps.

There were moments, rare dazzling moments, when he was not the cruel master she had come to know but instead, effortlessly charming. He smiled. He laughed. He asked her questions and listened patiently to her responses. And it was this man that she strived to please, this man that she desired, no, needed, to please, just as she strove not to disappoint the cruel sadist who took such pleasure in beating her. The sadist so willing to share her with Tomas simply to enjoy her humiliation and suffering. She accepted this as she accepted everything at the chateau – without complaint.

And then there was the Blue Room, that paradise of a bedroom on the second floor, where, once ensconced, Lily imagined she was not Darby's maid, to punish and please as he saw fit, but his lover. She longed for their nights there. The soft caress of expensive sheets against her flushed and naked skin. His magnificent body, naked and proud, as he stood at the foot of the bed. Those moments were enough to make her forget about the rest. Or at the very least, accept it as the price she had to pay to see this side of him. And she could close her eyes, lost in the pleasure he gave her, and imagined them not as master and servant, not as tormenter and tormented, but as lovers. As equals.

When he pushed her back on the bed, tying her to the bedposts, spread open for him, and feasted upon her sex like a man starved, burying his fingers in her cunt as he lapped that pulsing bundle of nerves, when he pushed his cock into her and played with her clit until she came, when he suckled her breasts, when he held her in his arms after a particularly draining bout of raw sexuality. In these moments, she felt loved. And happy.

She began to think of him not as Mr. Darby but as Edward, though she never dared to utter his name aloud. When they were together, he was always Sir.

Often, she was bound to the bed, unable to move, unable to fight off his advances, though she would never have fought him off, not in those almost tender moments of bliss.

If she learned to expect punishments when he summoned her to the Game Room, she learned also to expect pleasure in the Blue Room. Each room had a specific purpose and with it, a specific set of behaviors that he demanded of her.

He would, of course, tease and torment her. But she learned to love those teasing touches just as much as she loved the release that followed.

Under his expert tutelage, she learned to think of sex not as a singular act, but as an elaborately choreographed dance. A ritual. That each movement, though she could not always discern the reason, was done for a specific purpose. With a precise goal in mind. That he never explained his reasoning or methods did nothing to dampen her arousal. For wasn't uncertainty part of the allure?

For days at a time, he would refuse to let her orgasm. He would stroke her sex, working her up, and then, just as she thought he might give in and let her feel her release, his hand would drop away and she would be left panting. She begged. She pleaded. But there was nothing she could do or say that would make him change his mind once made.

On those days, he did not fuck her cunt for fear that she might take too much pleasure from it. Instead, he satisfied himself with her mouth or her anus. And she accepted this, knowing the pleasure that would come when he finally decided the time was right.

And so, after days of denial, days of wanting without receiving, of servicing without being serviced, when he announced over breakfast that he was expecting visitors that evening, she imagined that kind, charming man and curtsied, promising to be on her best behavior.

"We will need to find you something suitable to wear," he said thoughtfully. "As charming as I find your uniform, I think this occasion calls for something more…" he paused to light a cigarette, and blowing out smoke, added, "stimulating."

"Of course, sir," she said, unable to hide her excitement. He watched her, noting the smile, and returning it.

"Yes, I think I know just the thing." He checked the time on his watch. "Meet me in the Blue Room at five. Do not be late."

With that, she was dismissed. She shivered with anticipation.

At five, Lily stood at the door to the Blue Room, pulse elevated, nipples hard, cunt wet.

She was ready, as she always was, upon arriving here. For she knew what pleasures lived behind this door.

Edward, for he was truly Edward now, stood by the bed, his arms crossed over his broad chest as he waited for her to present herself. Wordlessly, she removed her clothing and sunk to the floor, feeling the hard wood dig into her knees. She inclined her head, waiting for him to speak.

She heard his heavy footsteps and then she peered at his shiny black shoes, so shiny that she could almost make out her reflection in them. She knew exactly what it took to get those shoes so shiny. For she was the one who shined them.

He stroked her hair in thought. She all but purred. Days of denial made her particularly complacent.

"Tonight you will not just be my servant," he said, his voice soft and gentle, "you will also be my lover."

Lily felt a swell of pleasure at hearing those words. Lover. A word she'd never expected him to utter aloud, no matter how many nights he came to her, no matter how many times she received him into her body.

It filled her with a strange, giddy pride.

"As such, I expect you to comport yourself

appropriately."

"Yes, sir." She would do anything to hear Edward, whom she thought of as hers, call her his lover again.

When he snapped his fingers, beckoning her to her feet, she heard none of his usual impatience. None of his usual irritation. She heard only that word, lover, ringing in her ears.

"Stand up and present yourself for my inspection."

A month before, she never would have imagined the grace and poise required to lay her body over the spanking bench. Nor the unexpected arousal the cool leather against her hands and knees could produce. In this position, her head down, she was completely accessible to him. Every orifice. He could manipulate her in any way that he saw fit. Could spank her, fuck her, take her mouth. He no longer tied her in place, knowing well she would not move from her position unless instructed.

He slapped her ass softly, playfully, and she felt her sex get hot and wet at the thought of what was to come.

"Tonight, you will serve my guests as you serve me," he said in a voice devoid of emotion. He stroked her behind and she struggled not to move, not to lean into his hand, knowing that it would only cause him to punish her for her wantonness.

"Tonight is a test. Do not fail me."

"I will do anything you ask. Anything at all."

He chuckled and she heard the affection in it. "I know."

He probed her sex with his fingers, finding her wet and ready for him. He probed her anus, using her arousal to lubricate her tightness. All the while, she remained motionless, taking short, even breaths.

Satisfied, he fetched something from the drawer and she trembled. Would he fuck her?

No. He'd want her eager when the time came. He'd want her dying with need, so hungry she would submit to any and all of his friends so long as he promised to pleasure her after. He would keep her on edge. Had he known they were coming for days and only now was telling her? Was that why it had been nearly a week since he'd last filled her cunt with his seed?

Without a word, he filled her ass with a large butt plug, stretching her completely and she bit her lip to keep from uttering a sound. Even now, she found her anus never fully prepared. But she did not complain, for as Edward had said, complaining was unbecoming, particularly for a girl of her station. He pushed and pulled and once satisfied the plug was well situated, he began spanking her firmly but without malice. She closed her eyes, focusing only on the sensation of his hand against her flesh, feeling it warm and pinken.

When he finished, she let out a contented sigh, wishing for more. But this was not for her, she knew, and so she allowed him to help her to her feet and then, the plug still filling her, he pointed to the bed.

There, laid out with the utmost care, was an elegant black evening gown. She looked up at him and he simply smiled at her and she felt that smile in her core, lighting her up.

It wasn't until he'd helped her into the dress that she realized why he'd selected it. The cool silk swirled around her body, making her feel sensual, elegant, glamorous, while the plunging neckline left little to the imagination. But the dress' real appeal, she realized, stepping forward, was that when she walked, the dress split open, in front and in back, exposing her almost to her sex.

She looked up at him, waiting for his approval. It came as a low growl deep in his throat, a feral animal let loose and she couldn't help but smile at the sound, pleased to know she had pleased him.

"Turn around," he said, almost lovingly and she obeyed and felt him lifting her hair. She felt the cool metal flush against her neck and then the click of a lock fastening it in place.

Without asking for permission, she lifted her hands, touching the metal collar encircling her slender neck.

He placed his hands on her hips and led her to the gilded mirror and she saw their reflection, the beautiful dress she was wearing and the collar, so perfect, so elegant, it almost brought a tear to her eye. Hanging from the center was a single lapis lazuli pendant, its rich color matching the wallpaper of the room almost perfectly.

"Thank you," she whispered.

"Don't thank me yet."

She heard the warning, clear in his voice. But she was too awed by the gift to be distracted by his ominous tone. Instead, she dropped to her knees, feeling the silky fabric part around her, leaving her sex exposed. "May I?" she asked coyly, lifting her eyes to meet his.

"By all means." He leaned back on his heels as she freed his heavy erection and began to kiss and lick it. She made love to his cock with her mouth, her tongue, her throat even, hoping that he could sense, in her devotion, the emotions welling inside her. He moaned, gripping her hair, forcing her to take him deeper and she opened her throat for him, welcoming his gift.

14

Darby instructed her to bathe before the guests arrived. She washed herself with the utmost care, and when she was through, she smoothed her skin with exotic lotion so that she smelled of rose petals. And her makeup, though subtle, emphasized her youthful glow. Her skin, so pale after a summer locked indoors, contrasted beautifully with the black silk.

She heard the first car arrive as she was crossing the large entry hall, the wheels grinding to a halt on the gravel outside.

Edward appeared beside her and pulled her against his chest. She breathed in his intoxicating aroma, masculine and clean, and smiled when his hand slipped up the slit in the back of her dress to caress her intimate folds. His touch was light and adoring. She sank against him and purred.

He withdrew his fingers, wet with her arousal, and presented them to her. Obediently, she sucked them into her mouth, no longer embarrassed by her taste.

"Kneel, my little flower."

The silk split around her, pooling on the tiled floor. With her knees spread, her naked sex would be visible to all who entered. She blushed, but not with embarrassment so much as passion.

She kept her head down demurely and waited. Outside, she could make out voices speaking, but not the words and when the door opened, she heard a delighted gasp.

They arrived in pairs, elegant couples who swept into the room with an air of entitlement radiating off them. Lily stole glances, captivated by their beauty, but she remained kneeling on the floor. She expected some comment, the cool caress of a stranger's hand, but nothing came. They ignored her, their lilting voices filling the air as they caught up with meaningless pleasantries, and with each passing minute, the color heightened in her naturally pale cheeks. For the first time since Edward announced he would be presenting her tonight as his lover, uncertainty gripped her. It reminded Lily of those first days and weeks at the chateau when she didn't know what she meant to him. When she could not discern if she was even to his liking.

She longed for his reassuring touch. For the comfort of his voice. Her excitement withered.

She was forgotten.

She'd imagined herself as part of the party, not on display, like a beautiful vase. She reminded herself that this was what Edward wanted and so, it was what she wanted as well.

When the final guests arrived, Edward snapped his fingers and she knew to follow them on her hands and knees. Down the long, narrow corridor that ended in the door to the Game Room. A fire burned in the hearth, the crackling logs giving the room a false warmth.

She had yet to see the faces of his visitors. She listened to their musical voices. Caught glimpses of gowns swirling across the floor. Of shoes, like Edward's, that gleamed in the low light. But she knew better than to raise her gaze and look at them in the face.

She wanted to make him proud.

She knelt beside the fireplace, feeling the heat of the flames licking her exposed skin. The need that threatened to undo her. The need to please him. The need to be pleased. And the uncertainty of being presented in such a manner.

In the Blue Room, when they were alone, he'd called her his lover. It was the first time he'd used such a word of endearment. But now, exposed and forgotten, she did not feel like his lover. She felt like his toy. His plaything. Discarded. Forgotten.

The pain it caused cut deep inside her.

The rejection worse than the most brutal beating she had received at his hand.

She breathed through her nose, even, deep breaths as she endeavored to appear calm and relaxed.

She heard ice cubes rattling musically against crystal glasses. Heard the hiss of a lighter, the burn of a cigarette. Laughter and voices but she barely followed the conversation, too distracted by her awareness of her nakedness. Her body.

How much time passed? She could not be certain. All she knew was that her muscles ached from holding this posture. Her back erect, her head bent, hands resting on her knees, her anus stretched and filled, her cunt wet, displayed and dying for attention. Each minute was an eternity. And then, Edward stood, resting his hand on her head.

She was reminded, once more, of a faithful dog.

A cold chill ran down her spine.

He cleared his throat. "As you all know, my little plaything came to me a virgin." Laughter filled the room, causing Lily's face to burn with shame. They all knew. Knew her secret. She had no secrets here, no privacy, but still, it felt like a violation. He continued, his voice placid. "I have rid her of that." More laughter. "She is inexperienced but she is not without her own charms. Enjoy her as if she were your own. She will not fight you. And if she does," he paused momentarily and Lily felt a cold sweat break across her skin, "you have my permission to punish her in any way you see fit. I ask only that you do not cause her any permanent harm."

With one final pat on her head, he strode off, leaving her defenseless. Exposed. She saw his shoes in front of her, as he came to sit on the sofa facing her. She could feel his eyes on her, judging her, waiting for her to defy him, to betray him in some way. Her muscles twitched but she held herself still.

"You may raise your head."

She blinked several times, composing herself, and then, carefully, she lifted her head and stared him straight in the eyes. His face was expressionless. Emotionless. Her lips parted. What had happened to the gentle lover she had been with this afternoon?

She begged him silently and she knew he could see it in her eyes, the fear, the betrayal, but if he felt anything, he showed nothing.

In that moment, her heart broke.

He snapped his fingers and a woman, a girl really, came to sit beside him on the couch. She was beautiful. With pale skin and dark waves that hung about her elegantly formed shoulders. She belonged of this world, Lily could see instantly. Of the same aristocratic stock as all of his companions, so unlike her, so perfect, and when the girl set her hand on Edward's muscular thigh, Lily felt it like a slap across her face.

The realization sank in. He wouldn't be content to merely share her. No, he would force her to watch him with this girl. Perhaps with all of the women in the room. Lily looked around helplessly. They were beautiful. Each and every one of them. Beautiful, distant, magical creatures.

She felt the bile rise to her throat as the woman stroked his growing erection through his pants. Lily wanted to scream, want to throw herself at his feet and beg for mercy, but she did nothing of the sort.

Instead, she remained motionless, kneeling on the floor.

All the while, Edward watched her closely, his expression so placid, so emotionless, it was like being stared at by a statue. Perfectly formed. Immobile. And cold. So very cold it brought goose bumps to her skin.

She shivered again and then she saw a flash of emerald out of the corner of her eye. A swirl of silk and then a woman was standing before her, leaning down, lifting her face in her hand, forcing her to look away from Edward.

"You've never been with a woman," the woman said with interest and Lily met her cold blue eyes, eyes like a winter lake, deep and glacial and unreadable. Lily recognized her, her voice, her perfect face. Brigitte. And she was once again afraid.

"I promise to be gentle." Lifting her skirt, she presented her sex to Lily, pressing it into her face and she could do nothing but attempt to please her, though the idea unsettled her.

She hated that the other woman was tending to Edward's needs and she hated that Edward was watching her submit to this stranger, but with tentative laps, she began licking the woman's naked cunt, tasting her, trying to please the woman as Edward had pleased her so many times.

She found the taste not entirely unpleasant.

The woman moaned, grinding her sex against Lily's mouth.

Distantly, Lily was aware of footsteps, of others approaching, crowding around her.

"We should move her."

"Don't be silly, she's doing splendidly."

"You're a selfish twat."

Cruel laughter.

"You'll get your turn. There's more than enough to go around."

Hands below her armpits pulled her to her feet, ripping her away from the woman's pussy. They carried her across the room, tossing her roughly across a bench.

It knocked the wind out of her. Her skirt split open. She felt the hard lapis lazuli dig into her sternum, a stone that only hours before had brought her such joy.

"I see you've started without me," a familiar voice said from the doorway and Lily felt her stomach knot with dread. She did not have to turn her head to know Charles

Dalton had arrived.

The same doctor who convinced Edward to keep her here when he'd wanted to throw her out. She didn't know if she should drop to his feet and thank him or curse him for the suffering she'd been subjected to.

Did she even have the right to call him Edward anymore, even within the privacy of her mind? It suddenly felt too familiar, too intimate, when he was passing her around like a cheap bottle of wine.

Or a common whore.

She lifted her eyes to see the woman, now draped across the gold settee, her lips around Edward's cock, and Edward's moan of pleasure, a sound Lily would recognize anywhere.

She did not struggle as her legs were forced roughly apart by the hands of a stranger. She felt resigned to her fate. Ashamed. Humiliated. But utterly incapable of fighting it.

Fingers probed her wet cunt. They were not gentle. They lacked finesse. They were not interested in her pleasure, merely in examining the goods offered to them. For that was what she was. A vessel. To be filled and fucked and tossed aside.

Someone twisted the butt plug and she cried out in discomfort.

"When was the last time she was allowed to orgasm?" Charles Dalton asked with almost clinical interest.

"A week, I believe."

"She must be dying for it."

Edward laughed. "She will do almost anything to come."

The truth in his statement made Lily want to die of

shame.

"Almost?" She heard the unmistakable interest in the doctor's question. "I wonder, what wouldn't she do?" he mused.

"You know the rules."

"They still apply?"

"They always apply," Edward responded tightly. Was it the doctor's question or the stranger's lips around his cock that made him sound so tense?

"Well, a man can always hope," the doctor said with a theatrical sigh.

"For the love of god, will you two stop bickering and let me have a taste of her," the emerald clad woman said impatiently.

"Brigitte, darling, you are such a brat."

"Charles, my pet, you are such a tired old bore."

The doctor laughed heartily.

"I'd very much like to witness her being defiled in all three holes at once," she heard Edward say and she wanted to cry out or pull away, but hand between her shoulder blades held her firmly down. She could move no more than an inch in any direction.

Edward's words from earlier echoed in her mind. Do not disappoint me. Never disappoint me.

She knew without looking at him that he was watching.

"I think that could be arranged."

She felt hot breath on her neck and she tried to pull away but the hand holding her down pushed harder. The bite of the lapis lazuli made her eyes water.

"You will take everything we give you and more, won't you my dear?" the same cruel voice said, causing her to whimper in genuine fear.

"For such an innocent, her cunt is sopping wet."

"She's a natural," was Edward's response.

The words stung like a brutal slap. Why was he being so cruel? He'd called her his lover. How could he treat her with such contempt, such meanness? When all she wanted was to please him. She'd have done anything he asked, anything at all, but why must he be so cruel? Why must he pretend that nothing that happened between them meant anything at all?

Unless, of course, it was all an act. Every moment of tenderness shared so that this final moment of humiliation was complete. Utter. Devastating. Lily knew he never acted without a reason. What if that had been the reason?

Luckily, she wasn't given time to consider this possibility. Without warning, a cock was shoved into her and she screamed out, unprepared for the sudden assault on her body. With the butt plug filling her back passage, her cunt was tighter than usual.

"Tight as a fucking vise. Well done, Edward," the owner of the cock commented. He fucked her with long, leisurely strokes, but even these subtle movements caused her to spasm.

"Yes, very nice indeed," another added, filling her mouth with his cock. She opened wide, too frightened to protest. All the while, from the corner of her eye, she saw Edward watching her. His eyes never left her face. Even now, she ached to please him.

Tonight was a test she dared not fail.

She moaned without meaning to, the pleasure of being filled finally, after so long, too much to bear. Even the cock invading her mouth could not fully muffle the sound, so clear to everyone in the room.

She loved this, though she hated it just the same. Love and hate the same in her mind. That which hurt was also that which brought the most pleasure. She'd had many nights, unfulfilled, unable to give herself release, to contemplate her situation. And that was the only answer she'd been able to come up with. That the pain gave the pleasure that delicious edge she craved and needed.

"Is she allowed to come?"

"What do you think?"

Someone pinched her nipples so hard she thought they'd be ripped off and whatever orgasm she'd hoped for died away. They wouldn't make it that easy on her.

They squeezed and tormented her nipples and then someone placed a clamp on her hard nipple, the sharp pain making her squeeze her eyes shut.

She was fucked, brutally. Ruthlessly. She let her body go soft, knowing that any attempt to fight them off would result in more pain and denial.

The cock in her mouth pushed deeper and then, without warning, she felt him come, deep in her throat and she swallowed around him, her throat convulsing.

With a wet popping noise, he withdrew and she sucked in a deep breath as she continued to be fucked, knowing that her respite would be short.

Every savage thrust made her breasts jiggle which in turn made the nipple clamps bite harder into her nipples.

The pain was exquisite.

She lost track of the number of cocks she sucked. Lost track of the number of times she was impaled. And finally, after what felt like an eternity, they stopped. Cum dripped down her thighs. She breathed through her mouth and nose, gulping air.

A bell rang.

"Dinner will now be served."

Lily buried her face in the bench, knowing Tomas, from his place by the door, could see the cum leaking from her well-used cunt.

She burned with shame. And yet, that dull ache between her thighs persisted. Unabated. Unsatisfied.

She needed to come. Needed it more than she had ever needed anything.

She needed Edward's touch. The gentleness that followed his most brutal punishments, when he would stroke her hair, restoring her to calm.

She did not move as the guests filed out of the room and then she felt a shadow fall over her, Edward towering next to her.

He crouched beside her, his hot breath on her ear. She turned her head to look at him, knowing he would see the tears in her eyes, and hoping that it would cause him to relent, though she knew it would do nothing of the sort.

"You did well," he said at last and she wanted to beg him to let her free. To put an end to her torture. But she knew there was no end in sight. He stroked the underside of her breasts with a gentle hand and then, without warning, yanked the nipple clamps from her abused nipples.

Pain shot through her and she did not try to stifle the scream that erupted from her lips.

He seemed satisfied by her reaction.

She wept in shame and pain and frustration. She wept, knowing he would have no mercy.

"Rest now. The evening has barely begun."

After dinner, they came for her. Edward dragged her limp body from the bench and pushed her to her knees and she submitted, thankful at least not to have to look his guests in the eyes.

"Get me hard and wet so that I may fuck Matilda in the ass," he said, pushing her head down on his cock, the cock she worshiped with her body and soul.

With a sickness in her stomach, she did as he commanded. Normally, she loved to feel him grow inside her mouth, loved to know that she was able to make him hard, that he desired her. But not tonight. Tonight, she knew that he would not use her as she desired.

And as she buried her nose in his pubic hair, taking him the way she knew that he liked, she felt someone part her skirt, exposing her sex, and then the brutal strike of a paddle against her naked flesh. She choked on his cock as tears sprung to her eyes.

She squeezed her eyes shut and focused only on Edward. She tried to forget the others, tried to forget the shame and humiliation she felt. Tried to ignore the strike of the paddle, the dull flat thud that echoed through the room.

Tomorrow, she would have trouble sitting. But tonight, all she could do was accept her fate as gracefully as possible.

She sucked his cock, hoping to make him come in her mouth so that he could not fuck the girl called Matilda. But Edward knew her too well. Roughly, he pushed her away as she tried, so desperately, to keep his cock in her mouth. For the first time all evening, she protested, clawing at him, trying to draw him back to her. Desperate. Frenzied. She couldn't bear to witness him fucking another woman. Not when he belonged to her.

But he didn't belong to her. She belonged to him. She knew the difference was more than syntax. If he wanted her to witness him defile another woman then that would be her fate.

She could, of course, get up and walk on trembling legs to the door, walk out of the house and never look back but that was as inconceivable as telling Edward to stop.

Her fingers tried desperately to grab hold of his pants, but he pushed her away easily, causing her to fall back painfully on her ass.

"Really, Edward, look at her," she heard the doctor say, a note of pity in his voice. "You should have done this ages ago."

She squeezed her eyes shut, trying to block out the scene unfolding around her. The rich and beautiful and she, their plaything. Their slut. Their whore.

"Girl," she heard Edward call out sharply. "Open your eyes and watch. Do not close them."

She opened her eyes to see Edward, standing naked before her, and Matilda, so beautiful, so stunning, so elegant, reclining on the sofa, a smug smile on her face as she glanced in Lily's direction.

Matilda's skin was perfectly pale, the color of cream. Just a hint of color adorned her cheeks, a flush of pleasure. Her dark hair fanned out elegantly around her. And yet, despite the innocence of her appearance, Lily knew not to be deceived. There was nothing innocent about the girl.

Edward rubbed her silky black pubic hair, and Matilda moaned theatrically and each moan, each sound of pleasure, was a dagger in Lily's chest, piercing her broken heart. Strong hands held her in place as she was forced to watch.

It was the doctor who pressed her down with his large hand between her shoulders.

"I think you've earned yourself a little pleasure as well," he whispered in her ear.

He manipulated her body and soon Lily found herself straddling his cock, her back pressed against his bare chest, as she was forced to watch Edward with Matilda.

And just as Edward pushed Matilda down and forced his cock between her ass, Lily felt the doctor begin to stroke her clit with expert fingers. With the fingers of a man who knew exactly how to manipulate her body.

She felt her arousal grow just as his cock swelled inside of her. She did not want the doctor to fuck her. He did not fuck her like the others. The others had taken her savagely. But the doctor was different. There was a quality to the way he moved inside of her that Lily could not define but it made her more nervous than the ruthless fucking of the others.

She fought her orgasm, not wanting to betray Edward this way. Did not want to be gently taken. Let them fuck her against her will, let them hold her down and torment her, but not this. Anything but this pleasure the doctor knew how to bestow effortlessly. He stroked her clit and massaged her tender breasts. She wanted to squeeze her eyes shut, but she knew she could not. Edward never looked away. Even as he pounded into Matilda, his dark eyes remained locked on hers.

Lily's sex was slick, hot, and her pleasure mounted just as her shame grew but the doctor was relentless with his caresses. And soon she found herself biting back her screams as she came, finally, for the first time in over a week. For while Edward may have feigned uncertainty about the last time he'd allowed Lily to orgasm, Lily knew down to the minute when he'd last given her such pleasure.

She had no doubt that Edward knew as well.

She kept her eyes opened as she watched Edward come deep inside the woman on the couch. She sobbed in silence, refusing to make a sound.

They continued to play with Lily for much of the night and she let them, resigned. At midnight, Edward glanced at the clock on the wall and announced that it was late and that he was tired. Snickers filled the room. He gave Lily a long, meaningful look then took Matilda's hand and left Lily to her fate.

The others paired off. And Lily found herself alone with the doctor. He was a gifted lover, his hands agile, as capable of causing pain with a flick of his wrist as they were of causing tremendous pleasure. Still, it was no consolation.

He pulled her, naked, to her feet and led her out to the veranda. Stars illuminated the sky and she held her arms around her body, freezing in the cold night air, as she stared at the constellations, trying to remember their names.

The doctor stood beside her, staring across the darkened yard and lit a cigarette.

He did not look at her when he spoke, but he didn't need to.

"Tonight isn't how you imagined it, is it?" he asked. She didn't answer which was all the answer he needed. It wasn't really a question. "I've known Darby a very long time. Do you remember when I told you about his wife?"

Somehow, in all that had happened since, Lily had nearly forgotten that it was the doctor who had informed her of this.

"Yes, of course."

"She was my sister," he said solemnly. "Stepsister. The daughter of my father's second wife. I came home from university and found her on my bed, this perfect little devil. She was fifteen at the time. And utterly frightening. Everyone loved her."

Something about the way he said this made Lily look at him quickly. In the darkness, his profile was barely visible. The light at the end of his cigarette burned bright.

"I knew Edward from university. He was like a brother to me long before he married my sister."

Lily didn't know why he was telling her this but she held her breath, not wanting to interrupt him. Not wanting him to stop.

He sipped his drink and let out a heavy sigh. "We all loved Naomi. It was impossible not to. When Edward married her, I don't know what I thought would happen. But I certainly didn't expect this."

"What do you mean?"

He turned and looked at her, and for a moment, Lily forgot the cold. His blue eyes gleamed in the night.

"She was the devil with the face of an angel," he said softly, turning away. "I should have known something would happen. We all should have known."

"How did she die?"

"They were sailing and she went for a swim one night. Never came back. We looked and looked but we couldn't find her. Her body was found by fishermen a week later.

She got tangled in their nets."

Lily gasped. It was a ghastly way to go, she thought, suddenly no longer preoccupied by her own suffering. That must have been terrible. For Edward. For Charles.

"There were a lot of people who blamed Edward for her death. Rumors circulated. That he had killed her." The doctor shook his head. "Sometimes I wonder if she knew exactly what she was doing that night. Everyone, even Edward, assumed she was drunk. But she had just turned thirty-five and hadn't taken well to the idea of getting older. I wonder if she did it on purpose. So she could die young and beautiful, a tragic end, rather than the slow slide towards death.

"Edward hasn't been the same since. He bought this house for her. She grew up not far from here, before our parents married. They would come here in the summers. Now, he doesn't leave."

"When did it happen?"

"Midsummer's, almost five years ago."

He dropped his cigarette, crushing it beneath his shoe. When they returned to the Game Room, they found it deserted. He had her sit with him for awhile on the couch and he stroked her thigh in an absentminded way that made her wonder if he was still thinking about his sister and what it must have been like to find her body, after a week at sea.

Something in the tenor of his voice made her wonder, also, if he had loved her in ways that a brother wasn't meant to love a sister.

At last, he kissed her cheek and bid her goodnight and she dragged herself up the stairs to her small bedroom, knowing that on the floor below, Edward was entangled in the perfect limbs of Matilda. It tortured her. But she was too exhausted from all that she had been put through to stay awake for long and luckily, sleep took her. But it brought her no relief. She dreamed of Edward and Matilda, locked in a tight embrace, kissing, making love.

When she woke in the morning, her pillow was damp with tears.

With a heavy heart, she forced herself from bed, still dressed in the tatters of last night's finery, and made her way to the bathroom.

Every muscle ached. And she could feel the dried cum still stuck to her skin, an unwelcomed reminder of all that had happened.

When she opened the bathroom door, perfumed steam rose to great her, enveloping her in its comforting embrace.

Sitting on the edge of the bath was Edward. He looked up when she came in, his eyes wide with a deep sadness that frightened Lily more than anything she'd ever known.

"Sir?"

He shook his head. "Don't call me that. Not today. Today, call me Edward."

Never once had he asked her to call him by his proper name and she felt a deep trepidation sink in.

"What are you doing here?" she asked.

"Shut the door," he said softly, "You're letting out all the steam."

She did. Enclosing herself in the large bathroom and hugging her arms across her chest. Last night, something changed. She didn't know what. But she knew, just as she knew that Edward knew, that some unperceivable shift had occurred without either of them asking for it.

Letting her call him by his given name was just another sign of it.

"Come here," he said softly, patting his thigh and she padded across the tiled floor and perched on his lap, carefully, because her behind stung from the beating she'd received at the hands of his guests.

He stroked her arms, his hands gentle and kind. And this kindness scared her more than the whip. More than the paddle.

She trembled and he felt her tremble and still, he rubbed her arms, warming her. She let her eyes close and breathed in the perfumed air. The scented oils that filled the bathtub. A lifetime ago, this would have seemed like paradise.

A lifetime ago, she might have imagined her wedding night like this. The perfumed steam. The tender caresses. The handsome man doting on her.

With hands so gentle, he turned her on his lap so that she faced him. He stroked her cheek with the pads of his thumbs. He brushed away the tears she hadn't realized she was crying. He whispered kindnesses to her.

"You came to me so innocent and pure. Just a wisp of a thing, trembling in the wind.

"I broke you. I took that innocence and corrupted it. And while it makes me a monster, I will never apologize for that. For taking you and making you mine." He gave her a melancholy smile. "I loved it. Loved destroying you. Breaking you. Corrupting you. And though it makes me a devil, I'd do it again, given the chance. I would do it again and again. Just for the pleasure of watching you mold to me. Watching you change before my eyes. Watching you become mine."

"Please, Edward…" His name stuck painfully in her throat.

He shook his head. "Hush, my girl." He brushed away another tear with his thumb. He pressed his lips to her cheek, but there was no passion there, no heat, only kindness. "Charles was right. He saw it long before I did. Because I didn't want to admit it. I didn't want to admit what I'd done."

She saw the pain in his eyes and she ached to soothe him the way that he soothed her, but she knew it was impossible. She waited for the worst to come.

"Last night was a test. A test you failed. Though you were spectacular in your failing." The words were said with such gentleness but they hurt more than a slap. More than a million slaps. "Tell me the truth. I won't be angry. Do you love me?"

Her mouth fell open in surprise. And yet, hearing him say it, she knew the truth. And she knew, also, that she must lie.

For the first time ever, she found herself lying to Edward. "No, sir."

He gave her a melancholy smile and stroked her cheek. "My little flower, don't lie. Not to me."

She sobbed as he held her, stroking her back. "I didn't want to see it. Didn't want to consider how your innocence might color our relationship. Charles warned me from the start but I didn't listen." With a heavy sigh, Edward added, "He was right."

"Please, sir," she begged into his shirt, knowing the worst had yet to come.

"He will come for you in the morning. And you will go with him willingly, because it is what I desire."

What last vestiges of pride broke inside of her. She sobbed. She begged and pleaded with him to reconsider but he would not waver. His mind was made.

"It is done."

She pushed out of his arms and sank to her knees before him, looking up, pleading with him. And he watched her, let her, did not stop her, nor did he relent.

"Today you must rest. Tomorrow will be very difficult."

She reached for his belt but he gently took her hands, stopping her and then he pulled her back to her feet. And then, with such gentleness, like he was handling a baby and not the woman he had beaten and broken so many times before, he undressed her and helped her into the bath.

She cried when he unclasped the lapis lazuli collar around her neck and slipped it into his pocket.

Warm water caressed her aching body, but she felt no relief. He washed her. Tended to her. And when he finished, when her hair was clean and free of tangles, he helped her from the bath and had her lean over the vanity as he rubbed scented lotion into her skin, soothing her pain.

It felt like a lifetime ago, when he told her she would beg him not to release her, and she had thought him crazy.

Now, knowing what was to come, she realized he had known her better than she ever knew herself. And she wept, knowing that he was releasing her. Casting her out when all she wanted was to stay, imprisoned here with him.

That night, sleep did not come. She stared at the crack in the ceiling, wishing he'd allowed her one final night in the Blue Room. But he did not. Instead, he sat with her for a few minutes as she drank a glass of brandy that he promised would help her sleep.

It did not help.

She envisioned a thousand ways to make him change his mind. She imagined chaining herself to the bed, refusing to go. She imagined hurting herself so that he would not send her away. She stared at the blue veins of her wrists, visible through her skin, knowing it was hopeless. He would only be angry with her for trying to change his mind.

When dawn crept through her window, she rose. Like a woman condemned, she dressed in silence, all the while hoping without hope that she would go downstairs to find him waiting for her. That he would tell her it was another test. Another torment to awaken his passion.

She knew that would not happen, though she hoped for it with all her body and all her soul. She'd seen it in his face the previous day. The determination. She hoped that he would change his mind and take her, struggling, fighting, to the Game Room, where he would do to her unspeakable things. Things she would love and hate with equal measure.

She did not weep. She was too tried to cry and anyway, tears could not convey the sadness, the loss, she felt.

Lily wandered the silent halls, the darkened corridors, knowing this would be her last chance to memorize every detail. Every sound and scent and memory that filled this place. This place that had become more than just her home.

She didn't trust that her memory would be able to hold it all. That in a month's time, she wouldn't be convinced it had all been a dream. Or worse, a nightmare.

She ached to see him, one final time, but he was nowhere to be found. And she did not dare knock on his bedroom door. Even after everything they'd shared, he'd never allowed her there. When she tried the door to the Game Room, she found it locked for the first time since she'd stumbled in and was caught. That fateful day that changed her life forever.

Feeling the locked doorknob beneath her hand told her all hope was lost. Just as that day he'd opened the door for her, hoping that she would stumble through it and into his arms.

In his office, where so many lashes had been delivered, so many punishments and pleasures, she stopped. His cigarettes, in their silver case, rested on the desk. She picked it up, and for the first time, she noticed his initials monogrammed into the silver case. She considered slipping it into her pocket and taking it as a souvenir. Something to remember him by. Something to remember this place existed. But she knew he would be upset and so, instead, though she had never smoked a cigarette in her life, she found herself unclasping the case and taking a cigarette between her fingers.

She lit the cigarette and coughed as smoke filled her lungs. But if she could not see him one final time, she wanted his scent to cling to her when she left and so, she smoked, though it made her ill. For he smoked.

When the car roared across the gravel outside, she felt a calm wash over her. There was nothing she could do but submit to her fate. And so, she went to the front hall and knelt before the door, her head bent, her eyes lowered, her knees spread so that her sex opened like a flower.

It was thus that the doctor found her.

He didn't touch her, but stood and stared at her a while. And then he cleared his throat and told her it was time to go. He held the door open for her and then, when she stepped out into the bright morning light, he locked it behind them.

She wanted to watch the house as they drove away, but as if sensing this, the doctor unzipped his pants and freed his cock. Looking at her, he did not need to speak for her to know what he expected. She lowered her lips, taking him in her mouth and she felt the car come to life and the gravel beneath the tires made the ride bumpy and she struggled to pleasure him. And in spite of herself, she felt her sex get wet.

Because Edward had trained her, and now, just sucking a cock, even the wrong cock, made her cunt respond.

She hated her body for this betrayal. For she did not want the doctor. She wanted Edward. Only Edward.

But Edward had forsaken her.

PART THREE

15

The doctor lived in a three-story mansion in the center of the village. Though only twenty-five kilometers from Chateau Oriol, Lily could not shake the feeling that she had travelled much, much farther.

From her seat in the car, she watched an old man step out of a picturesque bakery in the main square with a baguette tucked beneath his arm. How long had it been since she had witnessed such an ordinary act?

This return to civilization made everything that had happened in the two months prior feel like a dream.

"You will have more freedom here," Charles Dalton announced, ushering her into his spacious living room overlooking the town square. The room was decorated mostly in white, and the art on the walls, rather than the old oil portraits at the chateau, were splashes of color. Modern. Minimal.

Cold.

On the table sat a vase filled with yellow tulips.

"Sometimes it is freedom that allows you to best

appreciate your shackles."

Lily inclined her head, acknowledging that she'd heard. She hadn't uttered a word since her abrupt departure and now, here, she felt the weight of it settle heavily on her narrow shoulders.

Edward was gone.

After everything he'd done, she should have been overjoyed to be free. From her prison. For wasn't that what the chateau was? A gilded prison? Those stone walls designed not to keep people out, but to keep her in.

How many times had she wondered if Tomas' warning about wild boar and wolves roaming the property had been nothing more than another attempt to keep her from escaping.

Still, looking around at her clean, modern surroundings, Lily yearned to return to the comfort of those stone walls and the peaceful quiet of the chateau. To Edward, who despite his cruelty, had awakened her like a fairytale princess.

"I have a girl who helps around the house with the cooking and cleaning. Your duties will not be nearly as strenuous as they were at Darby's. You are free to explore the village. To come and go, almost as you please. However do not mistake that with actual freedom, my dear. Nor should you think it will make me any easier on you."

He lifted her chin with a finger, those cerulean eyes she'd once found so comforting now searing her. For a moment, they stared at each other. She could feel him assessing her and she stared back in defiance.

He was not Edward and she would not be afraid of him.

Satisfied, he dropped his finger from her chin, trailing it down her body. Her breath hitched. His lips quirked up in amusement as he cupped her breasts in his large hands, daring her to protest. She felt a familiar tug between her legs but refused to acknowledge it.

But the way her nipples beaded beneath his roaming hands told him all he needed to know. She was, as always, aroused.

He pinched her nipple cruelly between his fingers and she yelped in surprise.

"Better," he said, releasing her finally and she stumbled back. "In your room, you will find your things." He smiled, that same kind smile she remembered from their first meeting.

She'd thought this man would protect her, that he was an ally, a kind soul.

But that was only a mask he wore.

A mask he wore perfectly.

Cold fear snaked down her spine. He stepped back, slapping her firmly on the ass and she jumped, more in surprise than pain.

"Off you go. Your room is on the second floor and down the hall to your right. The door is open. I'll be waiting in the garden."

She was half-way out the door when he stopped her, saying, "And my dear, though Lily is a lovely name, while you're here, you will be called Belle."

She glanced over her shoulder and nodded. They had stripped her of her freedom. Stripped her of her virginity, her pride, her autonomy. Did it surprise her that they would also strip her of her name? That last vestige of the girl she'd once been.

But what was a name? Her mother named her Lily, but it was not a name given with love. Shedding it would not be such a terrible burden.

"Belle, hurry up. We have much to discuss."

Lily found a white summer dress on her bed. The room, so unlike the one at the chateau, was bright and large and pleasant. A large window overlooked the walled garden behind the house. Once changed, she looked at herself in the mirror and saw she looked like a porcelain doll. White dress. White knee high socks. Powder blue leather heels.

For a second, she wondered about that fifteen-year-old girl the doctor had come home to find sitting on his bed. Had she dressed like this too? Innocent and pure. But Lily shrugged off the image, not wanting to dwell on the woman Edward had once loved, and returned to the garden where she found the doctor reading the newspaper. The summer sun made his dirty blond hair shimmer like gold.

Lily was reminded of a blond angel in a religious painting she saw at the Prado so long ago.

"Sir."

"Belle *la bella*," he said, smiling and setting aside his newspaper. "Sit, please."

When she sat across from him, he tsked disapprovingly. "My dear, you mustn't have anything between your naked behind and your seat. Lift your skirt and sit down properly."

She had learned Edward's preferences so well they felt like her own. Now, she would have to learn to please another. It felt strange and unnatural, a betrayal even, but she did as he asked, lifting her ass off the chair and pulling up her skirt. When she sat again, the metal, hot from the sun, burned her abused bottom. She flinched without uttering a sound.

"Part your legs. You are, after all, here for my amusement. And I am not amused when your sex is closed up like a nunnery."

Again, she did as he requested, letting her legs part.

"Better. Tea?"

She shook her head but the doctor ignored her and poured a tall glass of iced tea, a subtle reminder that here, questions were never really questions.

"Drink."

She lifted the glass to her lips. Her time with Edward had taught her to obey commands without thought or complaint. The iced tea was just a hint sweet and soothed her parched throat.

The doctor frowned, his blue eyes turning suddenly serious. "The unfortunate truth is, you bore me."

Lily froze, the glass of tea poised at her lips. "What can I do?" she asked in sudden terror. What would happen if the doctor turned her away just as Edward had?

She couldn't go home. Not after her time here. Not after everything she had experienced, everything she had seen and done. How could she return to that tiny town she'd left behind? She'd always believed she didn't belong there, and if her time in the mountains had taught her anything, it was that she'd been correct. She wanted more. More than a small life in a small town. She'd gotten a taste of it at the chateau and she knew she wouldn't be satisfied with anything less.

And worse, what would Edward think if she failed to

please the doctor? She shivered. Even now disappointing Edward filled her with an unspeakable terror. She would not disappoint him, even if he could not see the ways in which she strove to please him.

Shrugging, the doctor said, "It's really not your fault. Some men like a woman who will blindly obey, who will submit without protest. I am not one of those men. I like a woman who will fight back. A woman with a little more bite to her. You, my darling Belle, are a kitten without her claws."

She opened her mouth to protest then closed it again causing him to laugh.

"See? We'll fix that, though. Don't worry." He rang a bell and moments later, a young woman appeared at the doorway. She was beautiful, her skin browned and freckled from the sun and her dark hair wild around her face.

"Yes?" She blinked her large brown eyes.

He spoke to her rapidly in Spanish as Lily looked on, wishing not for the first time, that she understood the language of the country where she now resided.

The young woman glanced in Lily's direction and Lily turned away and stared at the table in front of her, knowing instinctively that this servant girl knew the truth about Lily's position in the house.

That she understood, perhaps better than Lily even, the details of her servitude.

With a curious smile, the girl disappeared into the house and only then did Lily look over at the doctor.

"Did you know, in ancient times, they put ginger in a horse's rectum so it would hold its tail higher? It gave the horse the appearance of being younger and more spritely. Of course, it's illegal now, some nonsense about animal cruelty." The doctor winked at her. "What do you say? Shall we give it a try?"

Lily shook her head, pleading with her eyes that this not be her fate.

"I find it irksome that you never speak," the doctor said with a frown. "Different house, different master, different rules. If you have questions, ask. If you have doubts, speak. I actually find your provincial American accent quite amusing. So, tell me, my darling Belle, do you have any questions?"

For a moment, she forgot about the threat of the ginger. She leaned forward and when she placed her elbows on the table, the doctor chastised her. She pulled back hastily and asked the question that had tormented her since the day before. "Why did Edward send me here?"

The doctor cocked his head, considering her and she blushed, struggling to maintain his gaze when it was so deeply ingrained in her to lower her eyes. He had seen her undressed, had fucked her, had watched her crumble at the sight of Edward with another woman…he knew her inside and out. There would be no hiding from the doctor.

"I'm not God, you know. I do, occasionally, make mistakes. Edward wanted to send you packing and I told him not to. That's my responsibility. I hadn't properly considered how your *condition* might impact you."

Lily shook her head. "But what did I do wrong? I did everything he asked." Lily still couldn't comprehend Edward's motivation in sending her away. Why had he felt the need to crush her feelings so ruthlessly?

"You did nothing wrong. At least, not intentionally," the doctor said, patting Lily's hand. "It couldn't be helped, really. We should have realized what was happening earlier.

It would have saved a lot of trouble. For instance, we wouldn't be having this conversation now."

She shook her head in confusion. "But…"

"My darling girl, you are too young and too inexperienced for a man like Edward."

Lily's response was instinctual. She sat up straight and looking the doctor in the eyes blurted out four terrifying words. "But I love him."

For a moment, the doctor was silent. And then he burst out laughing.

"My dear girl, if you love him then I'm the Prince of Asturias." He gave her a playful wink. "I assure you, I'm no prince."

When she opened her mouth to protest, he just waved his hand dismissively at her.

"You haven't the faintest idea of the meaning of love. That's my fault. And so it is my responsibility to at least attempt to right the wrong that I've committed. You need to learn that Edward is not the only man in the world who can make you feel the way you feel. That the pleasure he gave you is nothing unique. And, for the love of all things holy, we must cure you of this foolish sentimentality."

The servant girl appeared with a large piece of ginger and a paring knife that she placed on the table before retreating once more. Curiosity laced with fear caused Lily to stare. She had learned, through Edward, that though she feared his actions, her body never failed to respond to the torture he subjected her to.

She craved it. Needed it. Desired it.

They had turned her into something terrible. But seeing the ginger, Lily sensed she would never again be aroused by the easy, uncomplicated romances that had once filled her head.

The doctor read her effortlessly. "You're wet, aren't you?" He began peeling the ginger with the sharp blade. "Just knowing I will hurt you makes your cunt flood." He flicked the knife with practiced, easy movements, causing the sharp, spicy aroma of ginger to fill the air.

Embarrassed but unable to lie, Lily told him the truth. She was aroused. But also afraid.

"That, my darling, is why I've decided to keep you. The world is filled with beautiful women. It's not your beauty that interests me."

With that, he returned to the task at hand. She watched as the ginger began to take shape. And to her horror, her body responded, her nipples hardening, her pussy throbbing as it rested, naked, against the hot metal chair. And the smell, sensual, exotic, was filled with dangerous promise.

When he finished, he held the ginger in the palm of his hand so that she could admire its familiar shape. The narrow tip, the flared base so that it could not get lost inside of her. Her lips trembled.

The doctor stood and held his hand out for Lily. She followed him nervously into the house, down narrow hallways decorated with bright artwork, and into the living room. It seemed so wrong, to be taken here, in this bright room filled with light and the peaceful chirping of birds. To Lily, such actions belonged solely in the shadowy rooms she'd left behind, hidden away from sight. Only now did Lily notice the small hooks and metal rings affixed throughout the room.

By the door, with her arms crossed over her chest, stood the pretty servant girl who watched Lily with bland interest. Lily's face turned crimson when she realized this girl would remain as a witness.

"Lean over the couch and present your ass for me."

Lily, obeying, pressed her palms into the sofa. She heard him snap his fingers and then the sharp click of the servant girl's heels as she crossed the room.

It was the servant girl, and not the doctor, who lifted her skirt and stroked her cunt with gentle fingers, causing Lily to whimper. How could she be so aroused by another woman? How could she enjoy this, knowing what was to come?

"You'll get used to the touch of a woman," the doctor said, as if reading her mind. "You may even grow to like it."

She'd expected to be shackled. But she was not so lucky. Instead, she was forced to hold herself in position so they might abuse her.

When the girl rubbed Lily's clit, she trembled with pleasure. How had she become this person, so willingly offering herself up to this man she did not love? This man who delighted in her screams?

Pleasure obliterated such thoughts. Her breathing grew shallow. Her pulse quickened. She was thankful, at least, that she was no longer made to wear the corset.

Cool lube trickled down the cleft of her ass and then the girl began probing her anus, stretching her with smooth, slender fingers. Without warning, she shoved the roughly cut ginger into Lily's stretched anus.

She gasped as it filled her narrow passage and her muscles clenched involuntarily around it. It didn't take long for the tingling to spread. Lily bit her lip in discomfort but uttered no sound.

"Get undressed," the doctor snapped impatiently.

With halting movements, Lily righted herself, feeling the plug inside her burn more savagely with each movement. The doctor and the servant girl watched her strip, their faces unreadable in the bright afternoon light.

In only the knee-high socks and heels, she stood before them and waited.

The burning intensified.

She squirmed in discomfort.

The doctor laughed. And then she noticed in his hands, the coil of rope. He beckoned her and she came to stand before him and he wrapped the rope around her hands before stringing it through a ring in the ceiling. Pulling on the rope, he stretched her body taut.

All the while, the servant girl knelt at her feet, wrapping rope around her ankles, and then she was forced to spread her legs. Thus, she was tied. Exposed. Stretched. And it was then, only then, that she felt the true burn of the ginger.

She felt like she was on fire.

"You really are quite magnificent." The doctor smiled as he stroked her cheek with false kindness. Her eyes widened in panic. The pain was unspeakable. Her insides were on fire. He trailed his hand down her body, exploring her flesh without hurry. He squeezed her nipples cruelly, until they ached. And then he pulled from his jacket pocket a pair of nipple clamps connected by a heavy looking chain. "And exceedingly determined not to make a sound. We will break you of that, do not worry."

The servant girl closed her hungry mouth around Lily's already hard nipple and licked and bit as Lily wept silently. Arousal coated her naked sex and inner thighs. She let her head fall back as the servant girl tended to her nipples, causing them to stand hard and tall. Lily moaned when she withdrew her warm, wet mouth and then cried out in pain when the doctor applied the nipple clamps.

"Edward may have punished you for your outbursts, but I will punish you for your silence. So, my darling Belle, I suggest you forget everything he taught you. Because if you do not fight me, your torment will only be worse."

Lily opened her mouth but could not bring herself to make a sound, even knowing that was what the doctor desired.

He clucked with disapproval and then spoke again to the servant girl. Lily heard a drawer open, and when she lifted her eyes, she watched the girl offer the doctor a wide wooden paddle. Lily tugged at the rope that held her arms so painfully stretched above her head, her natural instinct to cover her body, to hide herself, to run.

But she could not move.

She knew the pain that paddle could cause.

"Don't, please, don't," she sobbed.

The doctor smiled, cutting the air with the paddle, causing Lily to quake. Each stroke would force the plug deeper and cause her muscles to clench around it.

"This will improve you." He smiled brightly. "Embrace the pain and know that your pain pleases me. Scream, for your screams will please me."

He stood behind her and she squeezed her eyes shut. She jumped when he landed the paddle hard against her bottom.

"You will thank me for every strike."

She grunted as she accepted the second blow. "Thank you," she whispered through clenched jaws.

Again, he hit her. Again, she thanked him. With every strike, her muscles clenched about the plug, with every strike, her pain intensified. She struggled, trying to expel it. She was on fire. Every blow increased her pain.

And also the throbbing need between her legs.

She could not deny it. She was aroused. Painfully aroused.

"The joy," he said, delivering another forceful blow, "is not watching a weak woman submit but watching a strong woman give herself completely. So we must make you strong so that your submission has meaning."

By the fifteenth stroke of the paddle, she could not hold it in any longer. She screamed. Her lungs burned as her hoarse and desperate cries filled the room. The doctor did not stop. Between screams, she thanked him for every blow he delivered. She struggled helplessly against her bonds. Tears stained her beautiful face.

She would do anything to have him remove the ginger.

Even just for a second.

So she begged. She pleaded. She promised him anything and everything he could possibly want. But he did not stop. She howled in pain.

She squirmed, trying to avoid the strike of the paddle but it was useless. There was nothing she could do. No way to escape. She would accept her punishment as he desired.

"Cry louder!" he ordered.

And so she did.

"Fight me!"

And so she fought, every muscle in her body screaming in protest, but she pushed past it.

She struggled and tried to kick, though she was tied

fast. The rope dug painfully into her wrists and ankles but she struggled until her fatigued muscles could fight no more.

The paddle clattered to the floor and Lily dropped her chin to her chest and sucked in a deep breath as relief coursed through her. It was only then, hanging from the ropes that bound her, that she realized that her arousal was hot and burning between her legs.

Rather than cry silently as she was accustomed to, waiting for whatever Edward would grant her, whatever solace or torment, she begged the doctor for relief.

"Please, untie me. Fuck me. I need to come. Please." She sobbed for it, her shame dissolved by need. In her desperation, even the ginger was forgotten.

She cared only about the climax she felt she'd die without.

When the servant girl untied her, Lily collapsed at the doctor's feet and reached up for him, begging him still. He watched her, smiling, pleased with her pleas, but not enough to give her what she needed most.

"You must rest," he said, patting her head and walking out of the room.

The servant girl washed her and put her to bed and Lily whimpered when the cool sheets chafed her burning bottom. She did not protest when she was forced onto her stomach and then, her legs and arms tied to the posts of the bed.

The servant girl yanked the ginger from her abused ass and Lily sighed with relief but her relief was short lived, for the servant girl then filled her again with a hard glass butt plug.

Desire burned between her legs. Need consumed her.

She expected not to be able to sleep in such a desperate state, but within minutes, she was fast asleep.

16

Fingers stroked her sex and Lily moaned, rocking her hips.

"Ah, good, you're awake," the doctor said, withdrawing his fingers and she whimpered, wishing to feel them again inside of her. Turning her head on the pillow, she saw the doctor out of the corner of her eye. He lifted his fingers to his lips and sucked them clean before adding, "All in good time, my dear. We need to get you ready for tonight."

He untied her and told her to use the restroom. When she returned, he was sitting at the edge of her bed. She stared at him. This cruel man. This evil man. This man she found herself dying to please.

And he smiled back at her, patting the mattress beside him. She sat obediently.

"You did well this morning," he said, surprising her. "You fought beautifully."

"Thank you, sir."

He laughed. "You don't need to call me sir, though it does have a certain pleasant ring coming from you. Now, get dressed and meet me downstairs."

They ate dinner together at the long dining table while the servant girl attended them. How long had it been since Lily sat at a table and shared a meal with another person? Edward always insisted that she eat, alone, in the kitchen, another reminder of her status within the chateau.

It felt strange but not unpleasant. Her bottom hurt, but the chair was thankfully padded, and the pain was not terrible. And the food, oh the food, a delicious fish stew with a rich red broth tinged with paprika and garlic served with a crisp white wine.

Life with the doctor was not at all what she'd expected.

After this afternoon, she'd expected to be sent to the kitchen to eat as she was accustomed. Instead, they sat almost as equals, though Lily knew she was no more his equal than she had been Edward's.

Still, it was a pleasant change.

They ate in silence, giving Lily time to consider her situation. To contemplate what had happened to her. The doctor was nothing like Edward. Yes, they both delighted in causing pain, but that was all.

She thought about Edward. About the way he had taught her to please him, so that she did not even realize she was changing, shifting, morphing into the creature that he desired.

The doctor was more forceful in his demands but at the same time, less opaque. She was comforted, knowing he would tell her exactly what he wanted, rather than have her guess only to punish her for guessing wrong.

After the beautiful servant girl cleared their plates, they retired to the living room, where earlier, the doctor had tortured her so spectacularly. Lily couldn't shake the feeling it had happened to someone else.

She lifted her skirt and curled up on the comfortable armchair, tucking her legs beneath her, and sipped the brandy the doctor had poured her.

She knew, from the way that he watched her, that the time for quiet contemplation had ended.

She was not wrong.

"You are not only here to serve me," he said, lifting his drink to his lips and taking a small sip, watching her over the rim of his glass. His blue eyes seemed darker now. "You will also serve my friends. And I have many friends."

She nodded, too exhausted to fight him. If he said it, it must be so.

"That's it?" he asked, arching one eyebrow. "You don't have anything to say on the subject?"

She lifted one shoulder. "If that's what you want, I suppose it will happen whether I want it or not." She held his gaze and he smiled.

"You're not wrong."

"Why bother telling me? It's not like I have a say in the matter. Or do I?"

His lips twitched into a hint of a smile.

"I doubt you'd know what to do with yourself if you were given a choice. But you have a right to know what will happen to you. Within reason, of course. Sometimes it's the surprise that makes your reaction most authentic."

She cocked her head. "What do you mean?"

He opened his hands wide. "Desire is a varied thing. Some men like a woman to submit. Others, a woman who will dominate them. Some men want to take a woman by surprise, to feel her fear as she fights back. It all depends on the individual. And while I expect you to give yourself willingly to each and every one of them, I want your response to be authentic. And you, my dear, do not appear to be a very gifted actress."

She laughed.

"If I told you that tonight, I have a friend coming to town who would like a woman to satisfy his very particular needs, how would you respond?"

She blinked, surprised by his question. She was so accustomed to being told what to do that at first she didn't know how to respond. Finally, she stretched out her legs in front of her and yawned. "I might ask if these friends of yours are really friends or if they might be better described as clients."

For a moment, he held her inquisitive gaze and then he smiled. A true, radiant smile that made her once again realize just how handsome the doctor was.

"And I might say that you are more perceptive than you seem."

She held out her glass for him to refill, which he did with a flourish.

"Less hypothetically," she said, leaning back into the armchair, "what sort of particular interests does this gentleman have?"

The doctor lit a cigarette and exhaled a large cloud of smoke before nodding his head. "Yes, I think you'll do quite nicely here."

"That's not an answer."

He smiled, a wicked smile filled with sexual promise and mystery. "Ah, well, let's just say, some things are better left to the imagination."

They finished their drinks in silence. Lily tried to

imagine what sort of desires this friend of Charles might have, but she knew little aside from what she had learned with Edward and so, her mind returned again and again to the whip, the paddle, the restraints. She knew there must be more, but she could not imagine it.

Despite her initial reservations, Lily was beginning to think that perhaps living with the doctor wouldn't be all bad.

It wasn't that she liked the idea of being passed around. But there was something about the doctor. Not just his handsome appearance, though he was certainly handsome. But an openness that made her feel free.

Still, she ached for Edward. Ached for his touch. For the way he looked at her. She drowned her sorrow with brandy and the doctor let her.

When she reached for his cigarettes on the table, he said nothing.

"Is this friend of yours really coming?"

The doctor laughed and shook his head. "Not tonight, Belle. Not tonight. There's no reason to rush. We have all the time in the world."

She frowned. She'd been wet all day and other than the teasing of fingers, she'd yet to be satisfactorily penetrated. It disappointed her to think there would be no one to punish her tonight. No one to take her, use her, and hopefully, pleasure her as well.

She stretched out her legs and set her glass down on the side table. When she came to stand in front of the doctor, he looked at her in surprise, but did not say anything.

"Then it's time for me to go to bed." She cocked her head as she spoke and looked the doctor clear in his blue eyes. He had such beautiful blue eyes. She waited a moment before adding, "However, I'd prefer if you'd fuck me first."

She heard the challenge in her steady voice and wondered, her heart pounding in her chest, if she had just made a terrible mistake. Edward would never have tolerated such a bold request, but she was not with Edward. She was so accustomed to masking her desires, to letting Edward have her when and how he wanted, to being the object of his unpredictable whims, that she felt drunk on this new power, this unexpected freedom.

She reminded herself that she was not free. That this was just a show. Yet another elaborately choreographed scene.

But the rules were different here. And she wanted to see how far her freedom extended. More than anything, however, she wanted to be fucked. She wanted what he had promised with his actions this afternoon. With Edward gone, the doctor would have to do.

He stubbed out his cigarette in the ashtray and stood, forcing her to step back.

At last, he held out his hand and she placed hers in it and followed him, not to her bedroom, but to his.

She expected him to tie her to the bedposts. Expected him beat her. Instead, he undressed and lay down on the bed, his cock laying hard against his abdomen and curled his fingers, beckoning her.

"If this is what you want, take it."

Lily quivered with excitement.

He was not gentle but he was, without a doubt, very generous.

17

For the first time since arriving at the chateau, Lily had time.

Every morning, the servant girl arrived in her room and helped dress Lily for the day. There were silk sundresses and high-waisted skirts that emphasized her slender waist and the swell of her hips. The well-tailored clothing fit her to perfection and Lily was often amazed by how elegant she appeared. She was no longer the simple maid.

It was clear that the doctor spared no expense when it came to dressing her.

Once clothed, the servant girl would have her present herself, which entailed leaning over the foot of the bed, her legs spread, as she gripped the footboard. The servant girl would then stroke Lily's sex until she was wet and could not help but rock her hips, silently begging for release.

Some mornings, the girl would slide a pair of heavy metal balls into Lily's cunt. Others, it was a butt plug in her ass to keep her stretched and ready for the doctor.

Thus filled, Lily joined the doctor for breakfast in the garden. There, they drank coffee and ate pastries, all the while her wet sex pressed into the hot metal seat.

If the doctor did not feel like disciplining her then, Lily was free to wander the village. It excited her, knowing she was filled, her sex stretched, her anus invaded, her body a tool, a vessel, to be filled, as she walked through the sleepy mountain village.

The doctor's mansion was located in the main square, out of which ran cobbled streets. There was a pleasant café where she often sat at an outdoor table and read, knowing that if the doctor were to look out of the living room window, he would see her. The thought made her smile. She watched pigeons congregate around the central fountain. Watched the villagers gossip and go about their lives, completely unaware of the life lived behind the thick walls of the doctor's opulent home.

If the doctor joined her, which he often did, she watched the way the villagers looked at him, the respect so clear in their eyes as they tipped their hats in his direction. She wondered if they suspected anything about him. For how was it possible that he kept the life he led so perfectly secret and yet in plain view?

Her cunt was always wet when she returned to the doctor's home. And though she knew better than to pleasure herself, she thought about it often, at times she wondering if it wouldn't be worth the exquisite torture of a punishment.

Edward and the doctor had awakened something inside of her, something she had never suspected existed. All her life, she had been taught to think of sex as wicked. And the price of committing such a sin was weighty and inescapable.

She was the price her mother had had to pay.

But such thoughts belonged to a different life, one she'd left behind.

Now, she found they'd turned her into a wanton sex fiend. Her need threatened to destroy her, a constant, throbbing desire that left her limbs languorous, her skin flushed and her breasts heavy and tender.

Some mornings, after breakfast, the doctor brought her into his sumptuous living room, where, with the help of the beautiful young servant girl, he'd string her up and whip her. Or paddle her. She learned quickly to voice her pain just as she learned to voice her pleasure. She was no longer hesitant. No longer scared.

He gave her a voice. And while he did not always do as she begged, she learned that it was better to beg than to remain silent.

She grew to love these beatings. And the times when he brought her back to his bedroom and fucked her with wild abandon.

For the first week, the doctor had no visitors and so, at night, Lily would either visit the doctor in his bedroom before being sent back to her own room to sleep, or else, the doctor would steal into her room and take her, roughly, but always generously.

He never stayed the night. Lily didn't mind. He satisfied her sexually but he was not the man she wished to wake up to in the morning.

Lily looked forward to these brutal couplings. For while the doctor was not Edward, he at least satisfied her burning desire. And while he was beating her, while he was fucking her, she did not think of Edward. She thought only of the physical sensations overwhelming her body. In those moments, bound and abused, she felt truly free. Free of thought. Free of regret. Free of sorrow.

For otherwise, Edward was rarely out of her thoughts. She thought about the way he'd callously given her to the doctor. Of the way he'd humiliated her in front of his friends. And then, smiling, she'd remember the way he'd bathed her that final day at the chateau. The tenderness of his caresses. The gentleness in his eyes as he looked down upon her.

My little flower…

She thought she'd seen love in those dark eyes that haunted her still, but the way he'd tossed her aside as if she were nothing more than a meaningless plaything he'd grown tired and bored of caused her to doubt the feelings she'd once been certain he'd felt for her.

As if sensing her inner turmoil, the doctor kept her busy. And for that she would be eternally grateful.

On her eighth day, the doctor came to her instead of the servant and it was he who dressed her with the utmost care in a school girl uniform that made even Lily blush.

The red plaid skirt reached nearly to her knees. She wore white knee high socks and black patent leather shoes. And a white blouse tucked into the skirt. And around her neck, a short black tie.

She felt her pulse quicken as the doctor wordlessly fastened the knot around her neck. Tight but not restrictive. She waited for him to instruct her on what to do next.

Instead, he plaited her hair.

Finally, when he was satisfied with her appearance, he pulled from his pocket a pair of lacy white briefs and handed them to her.

"A man is coming this afternoon who has," he said, watching as she pulled on the panties, "as I'm certain you've deduced, an interest in girls of a certain type." He gave her a slow smile that made her heart beat faster. "He has certain expectations as far as that is concerned and you are to play the role faultlessly, though I have little doubt that he will find you more than satisfactory."

Lily nodded and righted her skirt. "What, exactly, does he expect?"

The doctor considered her and seemed pleased with what he saw. "He is the headmaster of an elite boarding school and you, dear Belle, have been terribly naughty. You must beg his forgiveness. And you must not give yourself to him willingly. It's the fight that he enjoys. Scratch. Bite. It's up to you."

Lily nodded. She was nervous, afraid to disappoint the doctor after all he'd done for her. "Is there anything else?"

The doctor shook his head. "I'm in the mood for a drive. Would you care to join me?"

The doctor drove a sleek, forest green two-seat convertible, and even Lily, who had no interest in cars, found it irresistible. She ran her hand lovingly over the hood.

Once seated in the cream-colored leather seat, she stretched her arms above her head, enjoying the warmth of the summer day.

The doctor, behind the wheel, looked perfectly content. He drove fast, assertively, weaving around the few cars they encountered on the beautiful mountain road. With the top down and the breeze blowing in her hair, she felt like she was flying.

They drove in silence and Lily forgot about the man who was to visit the house later, relaxing into the comfortable seat and watched the scenery pass. The mountains lush and green, but with a hint of danger. She saw the spire of a crumbling church in the distance. The hawks circling overhead. It was a wild place, dark and dangerous, untamed. She could easily imagine these roads in winter, covered in black ice and how easy it might be to careen off the edge and she wondered how long it would take for someone to find the wreckage.

But Lily knew she would never get to see these mountains in winter. By then, she would be back in America, back to the same routine of her old life. The familiar obligations. School. Family. She would be the dutiful student. The perfect girl she had always striven to be.

It filled her with sadness.

She must have dozed, because she awoke to the sound of the engine cutting and she sat up and blinked her eyes groggily.

"Where are we?"

The car was parked in a deserted clearing off a dirt road. All around them, tall pines loomed, casting shadows. Birds chirped.

"Having a picnic," the doctor said as if there was nothing odd about it.

He opened the door for her, and Lily stepped outside, her heels sinking into the soft, black earth. She considered removing them but did not want to ruin her white socks.

The doctor spread a blanket on the grass and Lily sat down, watching as he produced a wicker basket from the trunk. From it, he brought out a bottle of champagne, and he opened it with ease, the cork popping loudly, but without spilling a single drop.

He filled her glass and passed it to her and she took a sip of the cool liquid. It tasted delicious and she continued to take small sips as the doctor unloaded the wicker basket. Soft cheese and fresh bread, still warm from the bakery. Quince paste of such quality it was a deep, dark red. Fresh fruit. Slices of cured ham. While simple, everything was of the highest quality.

The doctor fed her as if she were a tiny bird, breaking off morsels of food that she ate from his fingers.

They ate and drank. She felt the affects of the champagne quickly and leaned back. When the doctor removed her shoes, she stretched her toes and smiled at him. And when he pushed up her skirt, she only lifted her hips to help him remove her panties.

He toyed with her sex with leisurely grace and expert fingers. She moaned with pleasure. Her cunt pulsed around his fingers as she stroked her heavy breasts.

He hoisted her up and positioned her on her hands and knees, her face pressed into the picnic blanket. She could smell the cool damp earth as he penetrated her forcefully. The champagne, the decadent food, the sensation of his cock stroking in and out of her, it all came together in a sensual glow that made her moan and swivel her hips, attempting to take him deeper.

He fucked her expertly and she came loudly, her body rolling with pleasure.

He bit her shoulder hard, causing her to scream, and then he came, filling her cunt with his semen.

Sated, she collapsed on the picnic blanket, still gasping

for air. The doctor gingerly pulled her panties up her legs and she lifted her hips. She could feel his semen dripping from her body, but she had grown accustomed to this sensation.

18

Lily awoke alone in the forest and when she glanced at the dirt path, she realized the doctor's car was gone. She shivered, hoping the doctor would not be gone long. The shadows across the ground had lengthened and she didn't like the idea of being alone after dark in the forest. Not with the beasts that roamed freely in these mountains.

Lily hugged her legs to her chest and waited. The silence was deafening. A twig cracked and Lily looked up sharply to find a man standing at the edge of the clearing, watching her. He was respectably dressed, his loafers spotless, his shirt pressed, but something about the way he watched her caused the hairs on her arms to stand up.

Lily stumbled to her feet, aware that her disheveled appearance would make it obvious what she'd been doing in this secluded clearing.

It never occurred to her that this might be the man that the doctor had mentioned that morning.

The man approached and Lily backed away.

He gave her a scornful look. "So this is what you've

been doing."

"My boyfriend will be back soon," Lily lied, hoping that the promise of a male companion would cause this man to back away. Instead, he stepped closer.

"Boyfriend?" He laughed. "You stupid little slut. You probably think any man you spread for is your boyfriend."

Lily recoiled as if struck.

"Students aren't supposed to leave the grounds. And for a tryst in the woods." The man shook his head in disgust. "I should expel you for this."

At last, Lily understood. Still, she trembled. The man watched her with eyes filled with such loathing, she found herself believing the lie. He grabbed her wrist forcefully and yanked her forward. Lily stumbled and gasped.

"Please don't expel me," she begged.

His sinister laughter filled the clearing as he dug his fingers painfully into her wrist.

"And why do you deserve special treatment when you've been nothing but trouble?"

Lily took a deep breath and looked up at him, making sure her eyes were wide and her lips parted. "Please, I'll do anything. But my parents…if I'm expelled…" she trailed off.

He pushed her down until her knees sunk into the soft earth. Her first thought was that she'd dirty her pristine white knee socks, but fear, genuine fear, eclipsed such trivial worries. For here, in the forest, no one would hear her. No one would come to her aid.

She looked up at the man, his face contorted. When he reached for his belt buckle, beginning to pull the belt free of the loops, Lily's fear turned to panic. She forgot the doctor, forgot her role as the naughty schoolgirl. She stumbled to her feet and ran. Branches slapped her face. Rocks and sticks cut at the soles of her feet, shredding her socks. She did not look where she was going. She did not feel pain as she ran as though her life depended on it.

She heard him crashing through the forest as he pursued her and she ran faster, pushed herself to the breaking point. Her lungs burned. Her muscles ached. Her feet seared with pain.

She ran like a woman possessed.

His fingers closed around her shoulder, yanking her short and she collapsed to the ground, sobbing between labored breaths. When she looked up at him between wet lashes, she saw he was breathing hard. She looked away quickly when he reached for his belt. She saw his erection tenting his trousers and knew what was coming next.

"Please, not this, anything but this."

"You should be thanking me for this opportunity. I could just expel you and then where would you go? Do you really think your parents would take you back?"

Lily cowered, certain that the man had no idea how close to home his words had struck.

He yanked her to her bruised feet, and she grimaced in pain. Dirt and tears stained her lovely face, but he did not care. He ripped open her shirt, causing buttons to fly through the air.

He turned her hard, forcing her against a tree. Rough bark chafed her delicate skin as he tied her there.

"Is this what you wanted?" he asked, forcing his erect cock into her cunt, already well lubricated with the doctor's semen. Lily wept as he fucked her, his thick cock stretching her wide. With her face pressed to the tree, she could see nothing but the forest floor and the trees that surrounded them.

Despite the dirt and the pain of the bark against her breasts, Lily could not deny the stirring she felt deep within. A single moan escaped her lips before the man emptied himself inside her.

Lily's white socks were stained with dirt when they returned to the clearing in silence. Her skin felt raw, welted by the sharp branches that had struck her during her run.

They found the doctor waiting for them, leaning against his sporty little car. He took one glance at Lily, her rough appearance, her shirt hanging open, her breasts and belly scraped, before turning to the man. As they exchanged pleasantries, Lily waited in silence. Her thighs sticky, twigs and leaves stuck in her hair. Lily hung her head to her chest. Finally, the man departed. The doctor wrapped his jacket around Lily's shoulders so that her appearance would not draw suspicion when they drove through the village, and helped her into the car.

The servant girl helped Lily into the bathroom, the doctor following close behind.

There, she bathed and tended to Lily's abraded skin, covering the welts in a thick, soothing salve. She brushed the knots from Lily's hair, removing pieces of twigs and leaves that had gotten tangled in her long blond hair.

The doctor, leaning against the doorjamb, watched in thoughtful silence. Lily was too exhausted to wonder if he was pleased with her behavior this afternoon. She let the girl take care of her, enjoying the small comfort that it brought her.

When she was clean, they brought her to her bedroom

and helped her into bed where she sank gratefully into the soft mattress. Her muscles ached. She felt beaten raw, not only physically, but mentally. Exhaustion made it difficult to keep her eyes open.

The servant girl undressed and Lily, despite her weariness, couldn't help but admire her perfect body. When the girl crawled into bed beside her, Lily accepted this without a sound. Pillowy breasts pressed against her back as the girl wrapped her arms around Lily's shaking body.

She cooed in her ear and Lily began, at last, to relax.

The doctor brushed her damp hair with his fingers. "It won't always be like that," he promised.

Lily nodded. And then, the girl beside her began caressing and stroking her and she let her eyes fall closed, relaxing into the sensual touches. The doctor stood by the door and watched as the girl brought Lily to a shuddering orgasm.

19

After that, visitors appeared most evenings. The doctor was true to his word. Though every experience was different, none were like that first time with the stranger in the forest. They would arrive early in the evening and sit with the doctor having a drink. Before their arrival, Lily bathed and changed into whatever clothing the doctor had selected for the evening. There appeared in her room sumptuous selections of lingerie. Silk that caressed her skin like a whisper. Delicate lace. Satin. Every piece was unique, every piece spectacular.

She never wore the same piece twice.

One evening, she wore a black basque that hugged her body and lifted her small but pert breasts so that her nipples nearly spilled over the top. With it, she wore a silk g-string and a garter belt and beautiful silk stockings.

While the doctor entertained his guest, Lily waited in her room to be summoned, sitting nervously at the edge of her bed. Waiting was always the worst part. Worse than submitting to strangers. Worse than the lashes of a crop.

She had long ago accepted that her body no longer belonged to her alone. That it was the doctor's, to share as he saw fit.

No, waiting, the anticipation, was what grated on her nerves. Who would she find in the living room? Who would she be given to this time?

In these torturous moments, she hoped, always, that it would be Edward, handsome, regal, cruel Edward, who would be seated next to the doctor. And though she was certain he would never come for her, every time she stepped into the living room and saw a stranger and not Edward, she felt her heart break once more.

She worried, too, that she would be forced to give herself to a man she found physically repulsive. But all of the doctor's friends seemed to be cut from the same expensive cloth – handsome, aristocratic, quietly powerful.

The servant girl arrived at Lily's door and held out her hand, inviting Lily to follow her.

They joined the men in the living room, hands held, and stood before them. Lily felt the stranger's clear green eyes appraising her. Like all the others, he was quietly handsome, with full lips and black hair that stone like the coat of a raven. He leaned forward in interest as the doctor sat back and sipped his whiskey. Lily never knew what to expect when the visitors came. Some wanted her alone, in her room. Some wanted a show.

The man cleared his throat. "Turn around, slowly, so I can see you."

Lily released the servant girl's warm, small hand and turned slowly in the dangerously high heels she wore, feeling his gaze burn her. She still felt nervous whenever they arrived. Like an inexperienced schoolgirl and not the woman she'd become under the doctor's firm, authoritative hand.

The men exchanged whispered words in voices too low for Lily to comprehend.

"Belle, he would like you to pleasure *minou,*" the doctor announced. He sometimes called the servant girl that, *minou,* causing Lily to wonder what their true relationship was. At times she felt like just another servant girl, at others she seemed more like the doctor's lover.

Lily shivered. For while she had grown accustomed to the servant girl's caresses, the way she toyed and teased Lily, seeming to enjoy it almost as much as the doctor did, Lily was still unsure when it came to touching the beautiful girl.

But she knew that she could not disappoint the doctor, particularly in front of a guest. The girl smiled encouragingly. Like Lily, she was dressed in exquisite lingerie. Burgundy silk and black lace adorned her tanned, lithe body.

It began with a kiss, slow and lingering. The girl's lips tasted of cinnamon. Lily closed her eyes and reached her hand around the girl, gripping her full bottom as she pulled her close and let her tongue explore the girl's mouth languidly.

Anticipation and nerves made her sex wet. She pulled away, biting the girl's full lower lip, eliciting a breathy moan.

It was a show. A dance. A slow seduction. She explored the girl's body, enjoying the way it came to life under her roving hands. Her hard, dark nipples reminded Lily of blackberries and she sucked them into her mouth, almost expecting them to taste just as sweet.

She knelt before the servant girl and pulled her panties to the side, breathing in the scent of her sex, heavy in the air. Lily knew the men were watching, but she forgot about them, captivated by the sight before her. She'd wondered if the girl's moans were all for show, but seeing her sex, ripe and ready, told Lily all she needed to know. That her touches excited this girl just as much as they excited Lily.

She feasted on her sex, licking and lapping, intoxicated by the girl's wild moans and the way her fingers tangled in Lily's hair, burying Lily's face in her hot sex.

When the servant girl came, her panting moans filling the room, Lily felt a sense of pride well up inside of her.

She knew she had done well.

And the sound of the doctor's slow clapping caused her to smile and lick her glistening lips.

The night was long. She was taken repeatedly, filled with the stranger's cock. Her cries filled the air, passionate cries of a woman being pleased.

In moments such as these, it was easy to forget the pain the doctor had caused her and feel only the way her body opened like a flower in bloom.

20

The doctor was not content to simply beat and fuck her. He strove to teach her. Learning to please the servant girl was only one of the many lessons he bestowed upon Lily during her time at his mansion.

One afternoon, as they relaxed in the living room, Lily naked, as she often was when in the house, the doctor snapped his fingers and Lily watched the servant girl, whose name she still did not know, shed her clothing and press her hands to the wall.

When the doctor produced a riding crop and held it out for Lily, she gave him a bewildered look.

"I doubt there's a dominant bone in your pretty little body, but that's not the point, now is it?" He smiled, caressing her cheek with his hand. "Hit her. Hard. Mark her."

Lily gripped the leather handle, amazed by how light the crop felt in her hand when she knew, from experience, the pain it could cause. The ease with which it could mark skin with bright red welts.

She gave it several tentative swipes. The faster it went, the louder the sound as it cut through the air. The girl quivered, bracing herself for each blow that never landed.

Lily looked once more at Charles for reassurance, and he smiled at her and simply nodded towards the girl.

"When you hit her, only strike the fleshy part of her bottom. Or the tops of her thighs. Do not hit her back."

Lily closed her eyes and swung the crop. In the silent room, the sound echoed loudly. She struck again, this time with her eyes opened, and watched the leather connect, causing the girl's flesh to ripple. The girl made a muffled sound, but Lily knew from experience that she had not hit her very hard.

She tried again, this time with more force and was satisfied when the girl yelped in genuine pain and her flesh turned a lovely shade of pink.

"Again," the doctor instructed and Lily hit the girl again. But try as she might, she could not get into the rhythm of it. She could not shake the awkwardness she felt. But she continued hitting the girl. Alternating between left and right, pleased each time the crop left its mark.

Sweat trickled down Lily's spine. She panted but did not stop.

Finally, Lily felt the doctor's strong fingers circle her wrist and he removed the riding crop from her hand and tossed it aside.

The girl's chest heaved but she kept her hands flat on the wall. Angry red welts marked her skin and Lily felt both sickened and a strange sense of pride. She had, at least, succeeded in marking her. She wondered if the marks would last, or if they would fade before long.

She hoped they would remain. There was a certain

majestic beauty to them.

"What would you like her to do now?" the doctor inquired as he stowed the riding crop in the cupboard where it was kept, hanging, with the whips and paddles.

Lily looked at the girl, could smell her arousal in the air, thick and heady. She was still so unaccustomed to making demands. It was one thing, asking the doctor, because she knew that ultimately all power remained in his hands. That anything else was a carefully crafted illusion.

This was different.

She hesitated before instructing the girl to turn around.

The girl looked at her, her lips parted, her nostrils flaring, her cheeks flushed, her eyes bright and Lily felt suddenly alive. The doctor had told her once that she would get used to being with women. That she might even grow to like it.

Now, as she sat on the couch and spread her legs wide and told the girl to pleasure her with her mouth, she realized that he had been right.

That night, at the dinner table, the doctor asked about her experience with the crop. Between sips of rich red wine and bites of meaty stew, she told him the truth.

"It felt unnatural."

He lifted one eyebrow, as if amused by her answer.

She held out her glass for him to refill while she considered her response. "It wasn't the physical demands of hitting her, though it was harder than I expected, but the options. Limitless options." She shook her head. "When anything is possible, how do you decide?"

The question was rhetorical but the doctor answered anyway. "For some people, power is intoxicating."

She shook her head. "I'm sure it is. But I didn't feel powerful. I felt…" she paused, trying to find exactly how she felt, "I felt anxious." She shook her head in frustration. "I didn't like it."

"Did you hate it?"

"No, but it's not something I'd like to do again."

This time the doctor gave a curt nod of understanding. "Many men enjoy being dominated by a beautiful woman. Especially one who looks as fragile as you."

Lily blushed. "I'm sure there are many beautiful women who enjoy dominating men."

"But you are not one of them." It wasn't a question.

"Are you really surprised?"

The doctor laughed. "Not in the slightest. But Belle, how could you have known for certain without giving it a try? You weren't given much of a choice in terms of your…" he paused, taking a sip of his wine, "awakening."

She blushed again.

"You'll be leaving us soon, it seemed only fair to give you as many opportunities as possible before that time arises."

Lily's heart sunk. It was easy to forget that there existed a world outside of this one, a world she would soon be returning to. She could not imagine a time when she did not live here with the doctor. For if she could not be with Edward, she wanted at least to remain with the doctor.

That night, as they sat in the living room after dinner, the doctor produced an unlabeled glass bottle from the locked cupboard and filled a delicate crystal glass.

When he handed it to her, she took it but did not sip it. Even without inclining her head, she could smell the liquor. Harsh. Astringent. Medicinal.

"Are you familiar with the story of Sleeping Beauty?" he asked settling back in his comfortable armchair.

Her eyebrows came together. "Of course."

"Tonight you have a very special visitor. He's always found that story to be most interesting. The idea of having a woman before him, helpless in sleep." He motioned to the glass she held. "Tonight you will take a sleeping draught. But unlike in that story, his kiss will not wake you. In fact, nothing he does will revive you."

Her hand trembled. "Will he hurt me?"

"No. Some things are forbidden, even in this house. He knows that he cannot harm you in any way. A pinch or a bite is permissible, but that is all. Even I have limits."

She glanced once more at the petite glass in her hand. The doctor must have recognized the trouble in her expression, because he leaned forward and patted her free hand.

"You will be fine, I promise. No harm will come to you."

For some reason, she believed him. She blinked her large blue eyes then swallowed the contents in a single gulp.

The bitter taste coated her tongue and she shuddered without complaint.

"Good girl. Now, it's time for bed."

Her room was filled with flowers and he watched as she changed into a transparent white silk chemise that grazed her thighs and made Lily think not of a fairytale but of a wedding night. She wondered what sort of man would want her this way. The innocent virgin, asleep in her bed, unable to protest.

She shivered.

The doctor pulled down the sheets and she crawled obediently into bed, the sleeping draught hitting her suddenly and she was thankful for the soft mattress and down duvet that enveloped her.

He kissed her softly on the lips. "Sleep well, *princesa.*"

The door shut softly and she lay in the darkness, waiting for sleep. She did not even feel it take her.

21

Lily awoke feeling more refreshed than she had in months. She stretched, amazed at the difference a good night's rest could have. And then, remembering what happened, the tiny glass of liquor, the doctor's promise, Lily ran to the mirror and there examined her reflection for any sign of what might have happened while she slept so soundly.

But there were no visible signs. No bite marks or scratches. Instead, her skin glowed a healthy pink.

Between her thighs, she felt her arousal and also her skin tight with dried cum, the only indication that what the doctor had told her was true. She blushed. Someone had been here, in this very room, with her. She closed her eyes and took a deep breath, trying to remember anything, some detail, some sliver of a memory, but it was a blank. She remembered only the doctor's goodnight kiss. Then darkness. A blissful sleep uninterrupted by dreams.

Lily followed the rich aroma of fresh coffee to the kitchen. There, the pretty servant girl was preparing a breakfast tray of freshly cut fruit. She smiled at Lily before going back to the task at hand and Lily poured herself a cup of coffee and took it with her to the garden.

The doctor was seated in his usual place, reading the newspaper.

Lily placed her coffee down, lifted her dress, and sat her naked bottom on the chair.

"How did you sleep?"

Lily yawned, the aftereffects of the drug still lingering in her system. "Wonderfully."

He nodded. "Yes, that cocktail is remarkable, isn't it?" He didn't wait for her response. "The man was very pleased with you. He said he will return soon."

Lily merely nodded. For the first time in a long while, her first thought was not of Mr. Darby.

Days passed as usual. The servant girl dressed her in the mornings. The doctor beat and fucked her. Strangers appeared and Lily greeted them on her knees. She welcomed them into her body. Her mouth. Her cunt. Her ass.

Lily found a certain languorous calm to their routine.

At night, she often went to the doctor's room. Some nights, the servant girl accompanied her. Some nights, she was alone with him.

Whenever the doctor produced the unlabeled glass bottle, Lily knew that the man who thought of her as sleeping beauty would be returning. She found she did not mind these visits for in the morning, she awoke so wonderfully refreshed.

The summer passed. The sun sank earlier each evening. Though it was only August, there was now a slight chill in the air that brought with it the promise of a brutal winter to come. Soon, it would be time for her to leave. The thought was inconceivable.

She felt, oddly enough, at home in the doctor's strange mansion. She thought regularly of Darby, but he no longer haunted her every waking moments. He remained, however, a shadowy constant, like a throbbing at her temples.

She was thankful for all the excitement. The visitors. The unexpected sensual delights.

For she still missed Darby. Missed the odd combination of tenderness and cruelty, missed his haunted estate, missed the smell of his cigarettes mingling in the air with the aroma of strong coffee. She missed the Blue Room, where they shared so many passionate nights. She fingered the hollow of her throat, trying to remember the feel of the lapis lazuli pendant resting there, but she could only remember the bite as it dug into her skin as she was held down and taken, repeatedly, by strangers.

Once, unable to hide her curiosity, she asked the doctor about him and he'd looked down his nose at her, almost in surprise.

"He's the same as usual," he'd responded cryptically before picking up a book and ignoring her for the rest of the afternoon.

She missed his skin. The scent of his body. His expressive eyes. He'd taken from her something precious, something no one else could take, and with it, he'd taken her heart.

As September drew closer, Lily could not shake the despair that her departure brought, the knowledge that she would leave these mountains and never see him again.

She thought, more than once, about hiring a taxi and going to him, but while the doctor allowed her certain freedoms, he provided her with only a few euros here and there, enough for coffee and a pastry, or chocolates, but certainly not for a taxi to Chateau Oriol. And she had no doubt that Mr. Darby would refuse to pay the fare if she were ever to try something so foolish.

Once, she'd thought of September with joy. Now, she hated the very idea of it. And every day that passed meant she was one day closer to leaving him forever. She could not hide her growing apprehension from the doctor, and Lily was thankful at times for his tact in not pushing her to explain her sudden lapses into silence.

"I'm going away on a business matter for a few days," the doctor announced one morning over breakfast as Lily sat impaled on the largest butt plug she had ever encountered. "*Minou* is coming with me."

She tilted her head in his direction but was too preoccupied with the enormous plug stretching her to engage in idle conversation.

"It wouldn't do to have you left alone," he said, cutting a slice of pastry and offering it to Lily. She shook her head. She wasn't the least bit hungry.

"And?"

"I know a vintner just a couple of hours from here. You will stay at his vineyard while I am gone."

Lily furrowed her brow. She disliked the idea of being left alone with a stranger. She knew, despite his penchant for her screams, that the doctor would always protect her from real harm. Even when she was alone, entertaining one of his friends, he was always within earshot and she knew, deep down, that if he had ever thought she was truly in danger, he would have come running.

In that way, he was like her knight. Her protector. He kept her safe.

"Finish breakfast and meet me at the car. Your bags have already been packed. And Belle," he said with a sweet smile that meant only one thing, "don't you dare remove that toy from your ass."

The trip, even with the doctor's expert driving, over rocky mountain roads, caused Lily considerable discomfort. She felt every bump in the road intimately. She gripped the cream leather seat, her jaw clenched, praying they would reach their destination soon.

By the time they arrived at the vineyard after several torturous hours of driving, she was sweating profusely and could not wait to be rid of the toy that impaled her.

The doctor, of course, had other plans. He had her lean over the hood of the car, in plain view of the enormous estate. The hood was hot and dusty from the long drive and it burned her skin where it touched her. He fucked her thoroughly, marking her as his. She had the strange feeling that this was a show for someone else. But whatever the purpose, she was not allowed to come. And when he finished, he took her bag from the trunk and placed it at her feet.

"The man you are staying with is very well-known and does not like for his identity to be found out. So when you're together, you will wear a mask. It's very important that you do not remove it and that you do everything he asks. I am a powerful man but there are men more powerful than even I."

For the first time in a long while, Lily felt true panic. The threat in the doctor's cautionary words was clear. He would not be able to protect her if she disobeyed.

The vineyard, in the dusty afternoon light, was perfect. Low crumbling walls surrounded row after row of green vines that grew from the red earth. The air smelled fresh and hot. Here it was still summer.

She was greeted at the front door and shown to her room where she was to remain until someone came for her. At last, she was able to remove the butt plug and she sighed with relief before taking it to the bathroom and washing it with soap and water.

Later, she was summoned. She placed the mask over her eyes, and followed a woman's voice down the hall, hearing their heels echo against the floor, and then she was ushered into a room.

She could hear the crackle of a fire nearby.

The man did not speak, but she could feel him watching her. She blinked behind her mask and waited. Finally, she felt his large hands on her body, his fingertips digging into her soft flesh. She fought the urge to pull away. The doctor's warning had stuck with her and she was afraid.

He tied her, standing, at the foot of the bed so that her arms and her legs were spread wide and she could not escape him.

His hot breath fanned her neck and she shivered in anticipation, her nipples suddenly hard despite the warmth of the room. His fingers trailed down her spine, causing the hairs on her neck to stand on end. His touch was light and filled with erotic promise. And with the mask blinding her, she could only imagine what he would do to her and wait.

The lashing he gave her was brutal. It set her skin on fire, burning and by the time he discarded his whip, she was panting, her sex dripping down her thighs.

She wanted nothing more than to be fucked, impaled on the hard cock she felt brush against her naked backside whenever he came in contact with her. But the man did not fuck her. He did not untie her. Instead, he stood on the bed in front of her and shoved his cock into her mouth.

She sucked him off hungrily. Ravenously. He gripped her hair, causing her to flinch as he brutally took her mouth. She obeyed with passion and lust, hoping that he would reward her later.

And just as she thought he would come down her throat, he pulled out. Hot semen splattered across her chest.

She heard him uncork a bottle of wine, the familiar chugging sound as he poured a glass. Her throat was parched and she hoped he would offer her some, or that he would untie her.

He did neither.

Lily did not know how long she remained there, tied to the bed, blindfolded, aroused, unfulfilled, but it must have been a good while, because when she returned to her room and removed her mask, the first pink light of dawn could be seen over the fields outside her window.

Lily remained at the vineyard for three days. When she was not with the man, she stayed in her room. She slept. She bathed. She wandered in circles. Once she tested the door, even though she had been warned not to venture out of her room, and found it locked.

Though she was never told she could not pleasure herself, she knew instinctively that she should not. So by the time the woman came for her, she burned with desire.

The second night was much like the first. The man did not speak. He did not address her in any way as he manipulated her body as he desired.

Again he tormented her. She begged him to fuck her, but he would only brush the head of his cock against her dripping sex before pulling away. This time, he did not even give her the pleasure of fucking her mouth. Instead, she listened to him grunt as he took his cock in his own hand while Lily pleaded with him to fuck her.

When he came across her belly, Lily cried in frustration.

On the third and final night at the vineyard, she felt a change in the air as soon as she entered the room, though she could not explain what it was that gave her that impression. A thick leather collar was fastened around her throat and he used it to pull her across the room and onto the bed.

There, he immobilized her with leather cords that dug into her wrists and ankles. He left her there, exposed, while he opened a bottle of wine, which he drank, no doubt watching her tremble in fear and arousal.

Every sound seemed magnified to Lily without the power of sight. She tried to imagine the man, what he looked like, what he sounded like, but nothing came into focus. She'd felt powerful muscles. The hair on his chest that brushed against her back when he pressed his body along hers. He was tall, that much she could tell. And very strong.

After two nights of torture, she expected more of the same and so she braced herself for a blow that never came. Instead, she felt his hot breath along her inner thighs, causing her to quiver as anticipation filled her.

He ran his rough tongue against her sensitive skin and nibbled her flesh. His stubble chafed her, but it was not a feeling she objected to.

When his hungry mouth hovered over her sex, Lily rocked her hips, inviting him to taste her, never expecting that he would.

Instead, he opened her sex with his fingers, finding a spot deep inside of her that he rubbed until she could not stifle her moans. Only then did he begin lapping at her sex, his fingers moving inside of her, his tongue on her clit, and she bucked and writhed as her pleasure escalated, threatening to pull her apart. After days of torment, it wouldn't take much to set her off.

She came loudly, her muscles clenching as she spasmed, her movements restricted by the leather cords that bound her in place and cut into her.

There was something almost familiar about the way that he had licked and pleasured her with his hands and mouth, but when he pressed his cock into her wet opening, she mewled with pleasure, all thoughts erased. He pounded into her, filling her. She felt his hand on her neck, his thumb pressing against the hollow of her throat, not hard enough to restrict her breathing, but enough to cause a flutter of excitement.

The man fucking her wielded his power expertly and Lily, beneath him, could do nothing but accept it, accept him, and with it, the exquisite pleasure he brought her. She came again, as he fucked her, her terrible shouts of pleasure filling the air.

She fell asleep tied to the bed and when she woke, her mask was gone and she was once more alone. She looked around the room and saw nothing that would give away the identity of her lover.

That afternoon, the doctor came for her.

22

Lily knew her time with the doctor was coming to an end, but neither Lily nor the doctor mentioned what would happen. Lily hoped that in not speaking of it, the doctor was tacitly agreeing to let her remain. For the thought of school, which had once excited her, now sounded impossibly bland. What, after all, could possibly compare to the excitement she'd experienced here?

And so, when the doctor beckoned her into his office, a room where she was never ordinarily permitted, and she found him sitting behind his desk looking grim, Lily knew the time had finally come.

She lifted her skirt and sat her bare bottom on the cool wooden chair and waited for him to deliver the bad news.

"Arrangements have been made for you to return home," the doctor said, leaning back and watching her. "You will, of course, be paid the money that is owed to you for your time with Edward."

Lily leaned forward, pulse racing, and shook her head. "I don't want his money."

The words were foolish, but they were all she had. She could not express how deeply hurt the idea of Edward, whom she'd pined for since he'd sent her away, paying her made her feel. It cheapened everything that they had shared. For while Edward had denied it, Lily knew deep in her heart that he could not be so callous, so unfeeling, as to have felt nothing.

The doctor laughed. "Don't be an idiot. It's unbecoming. Anyway, it's already done."

Lily stared at him. "When do I leave?"

"In a week."

"Don't make me go."

The doctor placed his hands flat on the desk and stared at them. "It's time. You can't stay here."

Lily shook her head. She felt the urge to cry and she buried it, refusing to be weak. "I could stay. I could clean or cook. I have nowhere to go."

"It's done." He waved his hand at the door. "You may leave now."

But Lily refused to budge from the chair, as if in getting up and walking out of his office, she was getting up and walking out of this life forever. The doctor considered her for a moment then shrugged.

"Suit yourself."

He went to work, ignoring Lily completely. When she still had not moved after several hours, sitting on her hands as she watched the doctor in grim determination, the doctor groaned impatiently.

"If this is really what you want," he said, a note of menace in his voice. Lily remained seated and when he tried to pull her to her feet, she fought him, clinging to the chair as though her life and very future depended on it.

But the doctor was much stronger than Lily and he was able to pull her, still fighting, from his office and drag her into the living room.

He tied her, naked, in the middle of the room and Lily quivered, watching him go to the cupboard. He selected a heavy whip, with knotted tails, and Lily knew it would hurt her terribly. But she did not want to leave and so, she did not regret her decision to disobey the doctor.

She expected him to whip her and delighted in the thought. But he gave her a knowing look and left her hanging there as he went in search of the servant girl.

Lily heard the doorbell ring. She was still strung up in the living room and she watched the servant girl answer the door and return to the living room with a man in tow.

The stranger gripped the servant girl by the neck and drew her lithe body against his and plundered her mouth. Lily watched, wishing his lips were on hers. They embraced like old lovers and Lily trembled with jealousy.

When the man released her, the girl knelt to the ground and Lily was forced to watch her suck the man's cock with expertise and hunger that could not be feigned. Lily's sex grew wet at the erotic display before her. How she longed to be the one on her knees. How she craved the brutal touch of a man.

They did not acknowledge her presence. Not once did the man look at her and it filled Lily with such desolation she wept.

She knew deep in her heart that this was the doctor's doing, that he had instructed them to pretend she was invisible.

The servant girl's moans filled the air, an erotic choral

piece that pierced Lily's heart.

She wished she could turn away, but she could not bring herself to even close her eyes. The girl's slender limbs stretched out, her muscles pulled taut. Pleasure rippled through her like a breeze on a calm pond.

Lily cursed the doctor bitterly. She cursed the servant girl and the stranger who pleasured her. Her muscles ached. Her body pulsed with unfulfilled need.

The doctor knew her well enough to know that worse than the whip, worse than the paddle, was this. To be ignored. To be returned to invisibility. The cruelty of it surprised even Lily.

Yet she did not regret her outburst earlier. How could she? When all she wanted was to remain here, in this house of sin and pleasure and pain?

Their cries of pleasure filled the room as Lily wept, forgotten.

23

"Get dressed. We're going for a drive."

Lily stared at the doctor, still seething from the night before. How could he have been so unfeeling? How could he know her so well as to know that was the worst torture she could imagine?

He sighed in irritation.

"Oh, come on, *princesa*. There's a sensible pair of trousers somewhere in your closet. And a blouse. Now, chop-chop, I don't have all day."

She hadn't worn pants since she first arrived at the Chateau Oriol so long ago. So much had changed since then that she could hardly believe she'd once been that that naïve little girl who arrived in the mountains without the slightest inkling of what would befall her.

The trousers were too long, and so Lily was forced to wear a pair of very high stilettos. These shoes, which once brought her so much discomfort, now felt like a natural extension of her body.

When she met the doctor in the living room, he

appraised her carefully and found her appearance satisfactory.

He turned on the stereo in the car and they drove, with the top down, in silence. Lily stared out at the landscape passing in a green blur, unable to believe that her time here was really nearly over. Months ago, she'd never thought she'd survive.

Now, she couldn't imagine life any other way.

They whizzed past the border and she breathed in the cool mountain air.

"Where are we going?" She angled her body to face him and he never took his eyes off the road.

"You'll see."

For a moment, Lily's panic returned. What if the doctor had decided, without consulting her, to give her to a friend?

What if this was the end? What if her outburst in his office had caused him to change his plans and she no longer had the last week she'd been promised?

"Please don't do this."

He took his eyes off the road for only a second. "Don't be silly, you'll be fine."

They arrived in the capital and he pulled his sporty little car over and killed the engine. They walked, hand in hand, into the opulent lobby of the Banc Nacional d'Andorra. The vaulted room, with its crystal chandeliers and oil paintings, momentarily distracted Lily from her troubles.

A handsome older gentleman approached them and Lily blushed, recognizing him instantly. How could she not? She'd spent a memorable evening tied to his bed.

But the man showed no outward sign of recognizing her. He held out his hand. "Daniel Soler. It's a pleasure to meet you properly." His handshake was firm, his hands soft and dry. "If you'd follow me."

She glanced at the doctor but he just smiled and waved her along. He remained behind, leaning against the marble counter adorned with brass.

Daniel Soler brought her to a magnificent office and when he closed the door behind them, Lily hesitated, unsure if she was expected to drop to her knees and wait for him to make his desires known. When he motioned instead to the chair, she was thrown off balance.

"Has Mr. Dalton explained anything to you?" he asked in that clipped, proper British accent.

"No, he hasn't explained anything."

The banker smiled. "He does have a dramatic flair, no? I've handled Mr. Dalton's finances for years. He's one of our premiere clients. There are a number of documents I will need you to sign before I can release any funds. We can transfer any sum to a bank of your choice, however, I do hope you'll consider continuing to bank with us. We offer certain," he paused, "advantages over other banks."

Lily shook her head. "I don't have any money."

"My darling girl," he said, laughing genteelly, "quite the contrary. You're rich." He pushed a document towards her and Lily stared at it. She saw beside her name an astronomical figure.

"This can't be right."

"I assure you, we do not make mistakes. Especially not of this magnitude. I will show you the safe deposit box when we are finished here."

Twenty minutes later, Daniel Soler led her to a small room off the main hall of the bank decorated in expensive furniture both ancient and regal and told her to make herself comfortable while he fetched her safe deposit box.

When he returned, he laid the metal safe deposit box on the table in front of her and offered her a glass of champagne to celebrate her sudden, as he put it, good fortune, which she accepted, more in shock than inclination.

"I'll be outside if you have any questions," he said before backing out of the room and closing the door noiselessly behind him.

Lily stared at the metal box for a long while before she was able to work up the courage to open it. Nothing could have prepared Lily for the sight. There, sitting atop neat stacks of money, was her passport. She picked it up gingerly. How many times had she wondered if Edward would ever return it, or if he intended on keeping her hostage in the chateau forever? She flipped it open and gazed at the single entry stamp from three months earlier.

Beneath it was another passport and when Lily opened it, she saw her picture, smiling brightly, and then the name, Belle Oriol. It listed her as a Spanish citizen.

Lily's mouth went dry. Suddenly, she was thankful that she'd accepted the glass of champagne. She took a large swallow before continuing to explore the contents of the box.

There were notes from various guests to the doctor's house, each accompanied by a gift, some small token of appreciation. A pair of diamond drop earrings. A silver cuff bracelet. The headmaster's note was accompanied by a first edition of *Villette* and she wondered if he was really the headmaster of an elite boarding school, or if it was also part of the fantasy that he craved.

She read each note, amazed by the tenderness expressed by each of the doctor's friends, and examined each present, but when she was finished, she put them all carefully back in the box. What use would any of this have once she returned to her old life?

Her heart nearly stopped when she emptied a small black velvet bag into her hand to find the necklace with the lapis lazuli pendant that Edward gifted her the night that everything changed. The night he gave her to his friends.

Sadness overwhelmed her and she found she needed to brush the tears from her eyes. She wasn't ready to say goodbye. Nor did she want to admit that her time here was finally over. But she knew that in bringing her here, the doctor was saying his final goodbye and making good on the payment promised by Edward, to be paid upon the completion of her time at the chateau.

Remembering the bank balance, she knew it was much, much more than they had agreed to.

She slid the necklace from Edward into her pocket, leaving the rest behind.

She noticed, at the bottom of the safe deposit box, a CD. A note tied to it read WATCH ME.

Curiosity piqued, Lily poked her head into the hall and asked Daniel Soler if there was some way she could watch the DVD. He was more than happy to oblige.

It felt strange to suddenly have someone serve her.

She stared at the television, her heart racing, sipping her champagne. Her fingers trembled when she finally hit play.

For a moment, the screen remained black and she worried it was broken. But just as she lifted herself from her seat, an image appeared and she sat down abruptly. There, on the screen, she saw her lifeless form, asleep in her bed at the doctor's, her blond hair fanned out on the pillow.

Her vulnerability shocked her. She looked so small, so fragile, in sleep. Was that how they perceived her always?

The door opened. And she saw him. Edward. Her heart stopped. For a moment, he stood in the doorway and watched her. Though the picture was grainy, she saw him squinting at her. He looked so serious. At last, he sat at the edge of her bed. Lily swallowed back bile. How could he have done this? How could he have visited her without informing her? This was worse than being filmed without her knowledge. Worse than the way he'd given her up.

The cruelty shocked her. She'd ached for him, weeping over his betrayal, his callous abandonment and now, to discover he had secretly satisfied himself with her unconscious body, filled her with inconsolable rage.

Never once had she considered the possibility that her nightly visitor was Edward.

She covered her mouth with her hands and watched him kiss her lips with such gentleness. It was hard to believe this was the same Edward she'd grown to know. She almost looked away, almost turned off the video, but she couldn't. How would she forgive herself for not knowing what happened?

By the time the screen went black, Lily was trembling. She drained the last of the champagne in her glass then quickly packed everything back into the safe deposit box, taking only the passports and some money.

The necklace was already in her pocket.

She shook hands with Daniel Soler and assured him

that she would continue to use his services. He beamed at her.

"I'm very pleased to hear that."

He accompanied her to the front door and when Lily looked around, searching for the doctor, she realized he was gone. Noticing her confusion, Daniel Soler informed her that the doctor had already left. And then he held out his hand and she saw in his palm a set of car keys.

"He wanted me to tell you that it was a pleasure knowing you," Daniel Soler said, giving her a mischievous wink. For no one else in this venerable room knew the truth of her relationship with these powerful, handsome and secretive men.

He lifted her hand to his lips and kissed it reverently. "I hope we'll meet again."

24

Lily pulled off her heels and tossed them onto the passenger seat before starting the car, feeling it come to life beneath her.

She was free.

She pulled on sunglasses and sped down the narrow streets, leaving the tiny capital city behind.

For two days, she drove with no destination. She thought about the plane ticket home but realized quickly that she had no intention of using it. She had no home to go back to. Silently, she thanked the doctor for the freedom he'd bestowed on her.

The first time she used her new bankcard, she held her breath, half-expecting it to be declined. Instead, the man behind the counter at the small hotel gave her a solicitous bow and thanked her profusely before showing her to her suite.

That night, alone in her hotel room, she thought about everything that had happened. The chateau. The doctor. Her passionate and savage awakening. She drank champagne. She slept in the luxurious bed, wearing a silk chemise she'd found in the bag of clothing the doctor had left in the trunk of the car.

She was free. Not just of the men who had held her captive for so long, but of everything. Of her past. Of her mother. She could disappear. She had a new name and endless amounts of money. If she chose, she could live a comfortable life without ever working again.

She spent two nights in the hotel, taking long bubble baths and relaxing on the bed. But the familiar itch returned and she could not remain still any longer. She packed her belongings and in the morning, she thanked the hotel owner and turned the car around and drove back to the village nestled in the mountains.

She located the doctor's mansion without incident and there she banged on the door, no doubt causing the neighbors to speculate. She did not care what they thought.

The servant girl opened the door and looked at her with surprise and Lily brushed past her.

"Ah, the beautiful Belle has returned. Was freedom not to your liking?" the doctor asked, crossing his arms over his chest.

"Where is he?" she demanded, ignoring his playful banter.

"So that's what brought our *princesa* back. He's exactly where you left him."

"I didn't leave him."

He considered her. "No, perhaps not."

"I don't have time for this. How do I get there?"

He laughed heartily. "It's easy."

He went to the table and drew her a detailed map. And

then, after a moment of hesitation, Lily wrapped her arms around the doctor and hugged him tight, surprised to find tears streaming down her face.

"What's this for?" he asked in genuine surprise.

"For everything," she said, brushing her tears away. "Thank you."

She drove recklessly. With little regard for the twisting roads. She wanted to be there. At the chateau. She needed to be there. To see him. If he rejected her again, let him do so in person, let him do so as he looked into her eyes and saw the pain he caused.

She cursed when she pulled up to the ornate wrought-iron gate, finding it locked. She wracked her brain, but she knew she did not know the combination that would open it.

She hit the intercom and she heard Tomas' smug voice. "Let me in!"

She expected him to ignore her. But to her surprise, the gate swung open. She sped around the drive and pulled up in front of the house, leaving the keys in the ignition.

The front door was unlocked and she burst inside, her bare feet slapping against the tiled floor. She knew she must look wild. Insane. Wearing the same clothing she'd been wearing when she'd left the doctor's days earlier. But none of that mattered. The only thing that mattered now was seeing him at last.

Confronting him.

She refused to be swept aside and forgotten. Not with what she now knew. Upon hearing his heavy, familiar footfalls, Lily sank to her knees, bowing her head respectfully as she waited.

She heard the sharp intake of breath and her heart pounded in her chest.

And then his hands, dragging her to her feet. She looked up at last, and saw him staring down at her, his face unreadable. Her lips quivered. But it was that handsome face that she remembered so well, that face that haunted her and filled her with longing.

"What are you doing here?" he asked roughly, his fingers digging into her arms. She felt nothing but overwhelming relief at seeing him at last. "I thought you'd run away the second you had the chance."

"I saw the video."

For a moment, he looked uncertain. Fear gripped her. What if he rejected her again? What if what she'd thought was love was in fact nothing but passion?

Lily's fears were unfounded. He gripped her by the back of the neck and pulled her close and claimed her mouth with his. She felt the kiss like an electric current coursing through her. Her body trembled. And she felt her sex get wet. She sagged against him.

He pulled away to kiss her face. Her eyelids, her nose, her forehead. He bathed her face in kisses and she felt her heart melt as relief overtook her.

"Why did you do it?" she asked.

"Do what?"

"Why did you send me away when I saw how you felt?"

He ran a hand through his hair and sighed wearily. "You're so young. So innocent. It wasn't fair."

She stood tall, her bare feet planted firm on the tiled floor and shook her head. "That wasn't your right to decide."

He looked at her in amazement. As if seeing her for the first time. How much she had changed without realizing? She thought fondly of the doctor. He gave her the strength to stand up to Edward, the strength to return to Chateau Oriol.

Had the doctor planned it all along? After all, he'd given her the chateau's name as a final parting gift. A last reminder.

But Edward, Edward hadn't witnessed her transformation. She had left him, a frightened girl, and returned a woman, willing to demand what was rightfully hers. She saw the realization in his eyes.

To Lily's amazement, he looked pleased.

"Maybe not," he answered finally. "But I had to try. You deserved your freedom. You know if you come back to me, I won't let you go again."

Lily gave him a radiant smile. "I have nowhere to go. So please, say it. Let me hear, just once, how you feel about me. And then I'll do anything you ask. Anything."

She thought for a moment that he wouldn't say anything. And then he gave her a lazy smile.

"Every night you were away was torture. Charles refused to let me see you. That was the only way. I'm sorry, but I couldn't go another second without seeing you. Without touching your perfect skin."

She felt safe and warm and protected here. With him. "I love you, too," she said with a shy smile.

This time, when he kissed her, all tenderness was gone. She felt his need. His frenzied passion, equal only to the passion she felt. Their time apart hadn't weakened what she felt for him. If anything, it gave her the distance she needed to realize just how deep her feelings ran.

This time, when she fell to her knees, Edward didn't stop her. She could feel the heat of his gaze scorch her. And the whole world ceased to exist.

"It was you, at the vineyard, wasn't it?"

The smile Edward gave her was all the answer she needed. Those three days of sexual torment, of uncertainty. The doctor had let her believe it was a stranger, someone too powerful to let her see his face.

Instead, it was Edward.

"I needed to have you. It wasn't enough taking you in sleep. I needed to feel and hear the way you responded to me. One last time before you left."

"How could I have left when you were here?"

He stared at her, his warm dark eyes admiring every inch of her.

"Do you have it?"

She reached into her pocket and held out the collar he had given her.

He took it wordlessly and then moved around her. With gentleness, he lifted her hair and then she felt it, the metal warmed by her thigh, as it wrapped around her slender neck. When she heard the clasp lock shut, she knew at last that she was finally home.

"Look at me."

She lifted her gaze and the sight of him before her, looking down at her with such adoration, made her skin flush with excitement.

"Don't be gentle," she said with a wicked smile. "Punish me. Hurt me. I'm yours. I'll always be yours."

He gave her a smile that made her heart race and then he snapped his fingers and she followed him, on hands and knees, to the Game Room where he'd punished her so many times before.

THE END

ABOUT THE AUTHOR

Katja Doremus is the pseudonym of contemporary romance author Katie Devoe. Inspired by a love of classic erotica, she explores the darker side of sensuality. She lives and writes where the inspiration takes her. For now, that's Los Angeles.

As Katie Devoe, she has published *The Stacks* series and *Gramercy Nights*.

www.ingramcontent.com/pod-product-compliance
Lightning Source LLC
Chambersburg PA
CBHW020608180626
46810CB00007B/2692